I0623132

Love on Lockdown

A Quarantine Romance

By

Amelia Kempton

Special thanks to

KM, HG, HW & AP

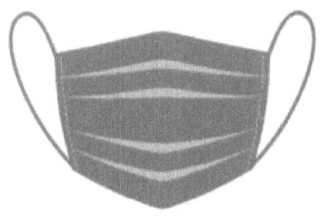

CHAPTER 1

Ivy watches a single tear fall down her cheek as she scowls at herself in her bathroom mirror. How did this become her life? Crying is quite common for her nowadays, but not usually so early in the morning.

She takes a few deep breaths and releases them slowly, attempting to calm herself. She grabs a makeup wipe to remove the mix of tears, mascara, and eyeshadow from under her eyes. Logically, she knows these are hormonal tears, not real tears. The awkward kiss-off texts she got from Gavin last night aren't the cause. They hadn't been seeing each other long enough to warrant early morning crying. The breakup, if you can even really call it that, was a slight disappointment at most.

Ivy manages to put some concealer under her eyes and slips her mascara into her pocket so she can reapply at work when her lashes will be dry. She arrives at work a little after 6AM.

First thing she does is move her chair to block the entrance of her cubicle. Ivy has been wearing a mask, but not everyone has. And management hasn't made it an official rule yet, so she's been creating a barricade to keep people away.

She puts her purse in her desk drawer and goes to her new adjustable standing desk. It figures that as soon as she finally receives her ergonomic evaluation and gets all her fancy new equipment, there is a global pandemic and rumors of not working at the office for a bit.

At this time of the morning, the small government office with its fluorescent lighting and stale air is still quiet. Only people with the longest commutes choose to come in this early, part of a constant strategy of dealing with Los Angeles traffic.

Not long after Ivy settles in, she hears Laverne arrive, rustling around a bit a few cubicles down. It will only be a matter of minutes before Laverne will come over to gossip. Probably ready to discuss the likelihood of us being able to work from home now that a nationwide emergency has been declared.

"Man, I love this traffic," Laverne says.

"It's pretty nice," Ivy agrees. "I wish it could always be like this. Minus the whole deadly worldwide plague thing."

Laverne snorts in amusement and then Ivy sees the moment Laverne sees her red puffy eyes. Ivy, once again, curses her damn perimenopausal hormones, the true culprit of inability to keep her damn tears in her damn head. Though certainly the stress of this looming pandemic hasn't helped.

Luckily, Laverne, who is usually very blunt, doesn't say anything about Ivy's appearance. Instead, they discuss what they have each heard about rumors of working from home and the likelihood of any state or federal mandates about everyone quarantining.

It's funny how quickly the countywide emails have gone from a general sort of, "There is a very low risk that this will become a thing, don't worry, keep working," to "Well shit. This might be bad."

Ivy would love to work from home, fancy new work desk be damned! She would gladly sit on her floor at home, her own personal laptop melting her lap if it meant avoiding sitting in traffic for two hours a day. Plus, hanging out in her pajamas all day with her dog? Maybe not even showering daily? Yes, please.

Not long into their conversation, a few more coworkers join in, all observing varying levels of physical distance, but nobody getting too close to Ivy due to her chair barricade. It soon becomes obvious that feelings about a stay in place order are divided.

One of her last coworkers to join the conversation begins to spout conservative talking points about the virus not being serious enough to shut down the economy and how people are overreacting, so Ivy goes back to her work, not too subtly slipping on her giant headphones.

The last thing she hears before she turns on her music is Laverne commenting that they will never be allowed to work from home and someone else replying, "If they don't want the government to completely shut down, they'll figure something out.

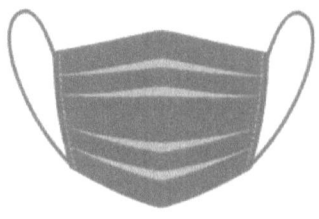

CHAPTER 2

"Come on, Toby. Come here. Come on."

Toby, the cutest, scruffiest little terrier on the planet sits on one side of the living room as Ivy stands at the other side, by the door, with his leash and harness in her hand. Ivy continues her attempt to lure Toby toward her, using her extra peppy tone she reserves for dogs and, on occasion, mockery.

"Come here. Come on," she continues, as she pats her generous thighs to encourage him to come closer.

It's not that Toby doesn't like going for walks- he loves them- but he's afraid of his harness. The same harness he has had most of his life, the same harness he is totally fine walking in once it's on, but the two seconds it takes to put it over his head keeps him sitting across the room, wagging his tail, just looking at her. Ivy switches to her stern, "Okay, cut the shit" voice.

"Toby. Get your ass over here. Come here!" And she emphasizes the command with a snap of her fingers then a forceful finger pointed to the ground.

Toby slowly moves toward her, his head down, behaving as though a beating is imminent despite never having been hit in his life. As he gets close to Ivy and she bends down to put his harness on him, he slinks back, just out of her reach.

This annoying dance is a daily occurrence. Technically, it is a four-times-a-day occurrence since each of their four daily walks begins this way. It's Toby's least endearing quality, by far.

Having successfully harnessed Toby, the two walk down the long hallway of their apartment building toward the front exit, Toby happily trotting, eager to get outside. They don't live in a fancy building. It's old, with minimal decorations or color in the hall or lobby, but it's clean and Ivy likes its 1940's charm.

She also likes the neighborhood; she appreciates that the building, which only has studio and one-bedroom apartments, seems to attract introverts like herself. Only one person in the building, Annie, is the sort to stop and have a conversation with people and Ivy has managed to avoid her for months now.

Ivy grabs a poop bag from the dispenser at the door, and they head out into the sun. Toby immediately takes a sharp right and heads to the tree a few feet from the front landing, sniffs, and lifts his leg to mark it. This will be the first of approximately three hundred million similar stops along their walk.

"Walk" is a less than accurate way to describe these ventures, but when Ivy tells people she is taking Toby for a "sniff and piss," she's often met with confusion and, if the person is not familiar with her sense of humor, there is a good chance of straight up offending them. So, Ivy has learned to sensor herself a bit around most people.

Their daily outings are a nice break in what has quickly become a very monotonous schedule. But daring to go outside is also odd because nobody seems quite sure if walks, when not absolutely necessary, are safe. Social protocols aren't entirely clear right now. Ivy wears her mask, tries to stay far away from people, and hopes she's not breaking any World Health Organization or CDC quarantine guidelines.

Due to the lockdown, Ivy has been working from home for over a month which has caused a lot of changes to her life. And for such a global tragedy, very few of them have been bad. The biggest positive change is getting to sleep in. Now that she doesn't have to be presentable at a certain time or make her commute, she no longer gets up at 4AM. Ivy considers herself to be a morning person, but that's a little too early, even for her.

The second big change to Ivy's daily schedule is that she can now walk Toby more often. Or perhaps more accurately, they can take longer walks and space them out better throughout the day. Even with her old schedule, she was often able to sneak in four walks, but one or two might only be walking from the front door of her building to the back, just enough for Toby to pee. These longer walks are a good opportunity to get out of the apartment and get back to a little sense of normalcy while, somehow, also becoming another element of this monotonous quarantine schedule.

Ivy has established about a half dozen paths they can take, all of which she has fully vetted, as to offer the fewest overall hazards. One route had to be abandoned the second time Ivy saw a dog off leash in its unfenced front yard. Another route had a blind driveway where the people who owned or visited the business rarely checked for pedestrians before just pulling out onto the sidewalk and tearing off down the street.

But what might appear to an outside observer as a casual stroll is never that for Ivy. She's always on high alert, only ever wearing one earbud so she can keep the other ear free to monitor their surroundings. No walk is truly relaxing for her, because she has a deeply held belief that the moment she lets her guard down, something bad will happen. Especially now.

Back home, Ivy wipes off Toby's paws, sets him down, and gives him a pet and a gentle smack on his bottom to signal he's free to trot away. Ivy takes off her shoes and her mask and proceeds to the kitchen to wash her hands and grab Toby's morning post-walk treat, his dental bone.

She sits down at her makeshift desk, a mélange of IKEA shelves, drawers, and storage cubes she had around the house which now form a large workspace in her closet. It's not the most structurally sound or most comfortable set up, but it's worked well enough for her transition to working from home.

Ivy logs back into her computer, catches up on emails, and gets back to work. She finds her job engaging enough, for the most part, but having worked various customer service or office jobs most of her life, she has certainly gained greater insight into why government does not function smoothly. No private company could run the way government does and still hope to stay in business.

As she works, she continues to listen to whatever she was enjoying on her walk- today it's the latest episode of *Stuff You Missed in History Class* and before she knows it, Toby quietly approaches to let her know that it's time for his dinner.

His presence takes a moment to detect since his usual M.O. for these reminders is to silently stare at her. From behind. And if she doesn't notice him after about five minutes, he will make a sound; something between a bark and a growl. It's his canine equivalent of a polite "hey!" and even though it is a little annoying, it's mostly super cute. Mostly. Especially since it's often followed by a twirl and a tail wag.

While Toby's internal clock is usually quite good, this time, he's thirty minutes early, but Ivy feeds him anyway because, goddamn it, he is too cute to ignore. She's a total pushover when it comes to Toby.

Not much later, Ivy's workday is done, and it's time for their third walk of the day. And this is how each day goes, with laundry and maybe a trip to the grocery store added in when needed.

Grocery shopping has never been her favorite chore but, she especially hates it now having to wait in line just to get inside. Then, dealing with the strange vibe inside where people are beginning to realize that supplies are limited and things could get ugly at any moment. Ivy goes as infrequently as possible. She was lucky enough to have picked up an eighteen pack of toilet paper before the panicked hoarding began, so she is at least set in that regard.

As Ivy and Toby step out of the apartment, she slips in her freshly charged earbud and resumes that day's podcast obsession. They walk down the long hallway and because Ivy is a nosy bitch, she tries to sneak a peek at any packages waiting for her neighbors.

She knows nothing about the people on her floor and she's fine with that. But it's fun to see what she can learn about them. Can she figure out their real names, not just the names she's given them? Maybe even discover their buying habits? Just whatever she can glean on a quick walk by.

Apartment three, AKA Messy Bun or Messy Bun With the Fucking Loud Yappy Dogs (her full title) does not have a package outside her door at the moment, but she has started leaving her shoes outside her door. In the common space. Which is against the rules and, frankly, just inconsiderate anyway.

It wouldn't be so bad if it were just *one* pair of shoes. But it's five. And they are hard-worn and just gross. Also, it's not a particularly wide hallway, the shoes get in the way if the delivery person has a cart or dolly.

Ivy couldn't help but notice that despite Messy Bun living alone, there are sometimes men's shoes mixed in with hers. Overnight. Ivy simultaneously thinks, "Good for her," and, "Should she be starting something during quarantine?"

Apartment six orders from Walmart a lot. At least weekly. So, her not-so-creative name is Walmart Woman. Ivy has no idea who lives in there but since there is a little beaded wreath on the door, she assumes it's a woman.

Apartment one has an Amazon package. Ivy's pretty sure that the lady who told her Toby is cute and so well-behaved lives there and so Ivy refers to her as Nice Lady or Lady With the Good Taste, even though her packages say Ramona.

After she and Toby are outside and no longer in the quiet hallway where her call would be disruptive, Ivy has Siri dial her bestie, Anthony. Of course, this simple command takes longer than it should because Ivy foolishly did not say Anthony's full name, so Siri is confused and replies, "I'm sorry, I don't see an Aunt Honey in your contacts."

Ivy tries to reply loud enough that Siri can hear, but quiet enough to not disturb her neighbors as she walks along the sidewalk under their windows. "No shit, Siri. I don't have an Aunt Honey. I said Anthony, you know, the person I call or text a million times a day? Fucking call Anthony."

"I'm sorry, I won't respond to that," Siri says in what Ivy feels is a passive aggressive tone, even though it is no different from her usual tone.

"No, I'm sorry, Siri," Ivy continues, genuinely wondering if it's weirder that she insulted her phone in the first place or that she felt the need to apologize after. "Can you please call Anthony Sanchez on his cell?" Ivy asks in an especially clear and sweet voice so she can still easily be heard through her mask. And Siri actually does what she was asked to do.

"Hello, dearest whore," Anthony says.

"Hello," Ivy replies in a happy sing-song voice, unoffended by this unconventional term of endearment. "How are you, you tawdry slut?"

"Have I mentioned how much I hate my job?" Anthony replies.

"Not today. But only because we haven't spoken yet."

"Well, then I'm glad you called so I can tell you today. I hate my job. How are you?"

"Oh fine," Ivy says, maintaining a cheery tone. "Toby and I are on our afternoon walk. And it is a lovely day, have you stepped out at all?"

"Nope. Just working."

"That sucks. Your work ethic is too good. Be like me and get an average paying job where you're just a tiny cog in a giant machine so that you could, potentially, just not work for one day a week and nobody would even notice!"

"That does sound nice."

"I know you're not done with work today, just wanted to say hi."

"Okay, hi. Thanks for calling. Nice to hear from you. I'm going to go kill myself now."

"Maybe try stepping into your backyard instead. You should be safe out there. Get a little fresh air."

"I'll step outside at some point today to play fetch with the dogs."

"Good. Get back to work you crazy slacker. Love you, joto!"

"Love you, bitch face. Bye."

"Byeeeeeeeeee," Ivy says, holding the "e" so long that it sounds like a dial tone. Anthony chuckles and then hangs up.

There are only a few people in Ivy's life whom she actually speaks to on the phone. She's not an animal for god's sake. It's only her sister, who lives in Colorado, and Anthony, who is like a brother to her. She would normally see him in person, but with his severe asthma, he's very strictly quarantining. So, quick daily calls are the new sad substitute.

As the call ends, the podcast she was listening to resumes immediately and Ivy's attention goes from one distraction to another, keeping her mind focused on happy fluff and away from reality.

Her attention drifts slightly from the chatting hosts to her new favorite brain-calming pastime, planning her dream home. This new obsession comes from spending an unprecedented amount of time at home. Now anytime she loads her laundry into her IKEA bag to take it downstairs to the laundry room, she can't help but think how her dream home will either have a laundry chute or just have the washer and dryer on the same level as the bedrooms. And why don't all bathrooms come standard with mini fridges to keep your facial lotions nice and cool?

Ivy used to walk Toby without listening to anything. But as her emotional preferences have changed due to the stress of the lockdown and life in general. Right now, she needs the noise. Even if she basically ignores whatever is playing in her ear, as she does now, she still needs it there in the background.

Multi-tasking with anything more complicated than doing chores around the house while listening to something used to annoy the crap out of her, but now? She finds that if she doesn't have at least one, often two things playing at the same time, she feels anxious.

In the evenings, Ivy has found herself on several occasions with the TV on while also scrolling through TikTok, a new addiction she has developed during her extensive time alone. Full volume on both.

When they arrive back home, Ivy wipes off Toby's paws, sets him down, and gives him a pet and a gentle smack on the bottom before he trots away. She takes off her shoes and her mask and proceeds to the kitchen to wash her hands and grab Toby's afternoon post-walk treat, his Kong filled with his incredibly expensive prescription wet food.

Having placed Toby's loaded Kong on his designated snack towel on the floor, in front of the TV, Ivy sits down on her couch and turns on Great British Baking Show and then opens TikTok on her phone. This is where she will stay until it's time for Toby's pre-bed walk. Then bed. Then it all starts over again tomorrow.

CHAPTER 3

Ivy has always considered herself a homebody, so being alone in her apartment night after night hasn't been as much of a challenge for her as it has for some. More accurately, Ivy was already a workweek and evening homebody. A very specific category of homebody she made up for herself.

Prior to the lockdown, she had a full social life, but only on the weekends. And most often, in the morning or early afternoon. She used to regularly try new breakfast spots with various friends, see a matinee with Anthony, or meet friends for coffee. And then, occasionally, she'd organize dinners with a bunch of the women she worked with years ago. On those days, she'd be home all morning and afternoon mentally preparing to be out socializing at night.

Ivy and a friend even established FreCreamTe Saturdays, where every few Saturdays they would try a new place that had good French toast, then get ice-cream, and have a latte. These three items could be obtained at the same place or separate locations, just as long as all three were consumed. Ivy created a theme song for the day which she would sing as they drove to their destinations, and which her friend would indulgently bob her head along to, never joining in on the singing.

Unfortunately, they were only able to enjoy a handful of FreCreamTe Saturdays before the lockdown. Now, Ivy would kill for a latte that was not from a drive thru.

On their first long walk (second actual walk of the day) Ivy and Toby head toward the park to see if it's open again. The gates have been locked for a while with signs from the city explaining that the park would be closed indefinitely due to COVID restrictions.

As they round the corner, Toby's attention is grabbed by Hildy, a little chihuahua mix who lives in the apartment building across the street. Her owner, Otto, follows her with his camera, placed at the end of a long selfie stick. Hildy is the star of her own YouTube channel, Hildy TV. Otto records their walks and features the many dogs they encounter in the neighborhood. Hildy's guest stars have really plummeted during lockdown, most of her videos now only consisting of her walking alone.

Otto does still try to recruit people to allow their dogs to be filmed, there are just far fewer people out with their dogs to ask. Ivy isn't sure how much of this should still be allowed right now, but somehow Otto's determination to continue during quarantine is comforting to her, so she and Toby cross the street to join Hildy on her walk.

"Toby!" Otto calls out, with genuine excitement, as he shifts the camera from Hildy to Toby. Otto reaches down and attempts to pet Toby, as he does each time he sees him, and just like every other time, Toby backs away in a manner that probably makes people think he is abused at home. (He is not. He is spoiled as hell.)

Ivy once explained to Otto that Toby is like a stripper, he can touch you, but you can't touch him, but Otto reacted to that analogy in the same way many people who don't really know her react to the shit she says: just a complete lack of acknowledgment that she is joking and a desire to move on to a new topic.

The four of them stroll down the street. Whenever Ivy walks with Otto, she can't help but think they look like two of the three hitchhiking ghosts from the Haunted Mansion ride. Otto is Ezra, the tall, skeletal one and Ivy is Phineas, the fat one. They just need to find a Gus, a little bearded man to walk around with them and complete the trio.

Otto and Ivy maintain their distance and wear masks, though Otto's often slips off his nose as they walk to the park, which is indeed closed. As they head back home, Otto talks about the dogs he has managed to film recently, how many new videos he has posted, and how good he's getting at editing.

Ivy makes another mental note to actually watch the videos he keeps raving about. At least the ones Toby is in. And of course, to give them a "like", something Otto emphasizes every time he mentions the channel.

As Ivy's tolerance of banal chitchat reaches its limit, she begins to subtly guide Toby down a side street, a route Otto and Hildy don't tend to take.

Her escape is made easier by the arrival of a woman who appears to have also come by to see if the park was open yet and who is walking an adorable puppy. Otto determinedly goes to film the little fluffball, Toby and Ivy forgotten.

Ivy takes Toby on one of their longer paths since the weather is so nice and cool and Toby is actually walking this time, not just sniffing.

Back home, Ivy wipes down Toby's paws, sets him down, and gives him his pet and a gentle smack on the bottom before he trots away. She takes off her shoes and her mask and proceeds to the kitchen to wash her hands and grab Toby's morning post-walk treat, his dental bone.

She sits down at her desk to focus on work until Toby lets her know it is time for his dinner. And the rest of the day continues as all the previous days of the last month and a half.

<u>CHAPTER 4</u>

Later that week, Ivy and Toby walk down to the park to find that one of the entrances is open. A new sign with social distancing and masking guidelines is next to the entrance now. As they walk through the gates, Ivy sees caution tape around the playground, the swings having been wound around the top pole so nobody can use them. There's a warning sign taped over the park sign. Ivy's too far away to read the details, but it likely has the same sort social distancing recommendations the other signs have.

As they walk further into the park, Ivy sees Otto standing a safe distance from a dark haired man and his dog. Otto films the little gray poodle who Hildy is sniffing with only mild interest.

The lack of energy between the two is not creating the sort of content Hildy's followers are looking for, so when Otto spots Toby, he gestures for Ivy to bring him over. This was unnecessary since Toby began pulling Ivy towards Hildy the moment he saw her.

As they make their way over to the men, Ivy gives the mystery man a better look. He's not as tall as Otto, who is well over six foot, but he is still tall. Taller than her. He also has a full head of thick, dark, wavey hair and full but tamed eyebrows; the type of brows that suggest the man must pluck or wax them to keep them separated. His big brown eyes seem friendly. The rest of his face is, of course, covered by a blue surgical mask.

"Hi," Ivy says to both Otto and the man. She watches Toby try to approach Hildy, but Hildy, who is rarely on a leash, easily avoids him. Thwarted, Toby then takes a moment to sniff the poodle instead.

"Oh these two must be good friends," Otto says, watching Toby wag his tail excitedly at the poodle. Toby's large ears are pointed straight up as he sniffs his new friend. Ivy calls these Toby's "horny ears" because he usually gets them when meeting new female dogs, but she's never told Otto that, for obvious reasons.

"No, just an instant love connection, I guess," Ivy says.

"But they're neighbors! You two know each other, right?" Otto says, as he gestures between Ivy and the man. "You live in the same building."

"No," says the man. "I don't think we've met, but it is kind of hard to tell in these things," and he points to the mask he wears, properly, over his nose and mouth. Like a decent human being. "I'm Jason," he continues, as he does a quick awkward wave, the new replacement to a handshake.

"Hi, I'm Ivy," she says as she returns the wave. "Are you new to the building?"

"No, I've been there . . ." he pauses briefly as if he's doing mental calculations, "over a year now, I guess. Maybe two? You?"

"Almost four. Do you live on the second floor?"

"I do, actually," he replies with a tone like someone who has just had a psychic tell them some bit of unexpectedly accurate information about themselves.

"That would explain it. There's no reason for me to go up there, so all of you are a mystery to me."

"Yah, that's too bad. We're all really great on the second floor. Well, the *top* floor. That's what we 'toppies' call it."

Ivy smiles, appreciating his offbeat humor, similar to her own. Then she remembers that he can't see that she's smiling. "Oh yes," she says, "The elite. I'm just a ground floor flunky."

"Well at least you aren't one of the basement monsters," Jason replies.

"Yuck, never. Can you imagine?"

Ivy is enjoying their exchange but realizes that Otto has no idea what she and Jason are talking about and that he's just sort of staring at each of them in turn.

"So," Ivy says, "Who is this?" She points at the poodle who has started to wander off, but at such a painfully slow pace that Jason doesn't appear to be concerned.

"That's Harry," Jason says.

"Harry is eighteen, can you believe it?" Otto remarks.

Ivy can easily believe it. Harry is giving off Crypt-Keeper vibes. But what she says is, "That's impressive. I hope Toby lives that long."

"Toby must be about four, he's got plenty of years ahead of him," Otto says, in a tone meant to illustrate the dog-related wisdom he has gained from his seventy years on the planet.

"He's actually nine," says Ivy. "I like to take the fact that he still looks young as a reflection of my good dog-ownership. But it's probably just genetics."

Harry continues his wobbly journey toward the park gates and has gotten far enough away now that Jason takes the hint. "We'd better head back home. I think Harry has been out long enough." And looking at Ivy he says, "Nice to meet you," and Ivy pictures a warm smile under his mask.

Jason nods his head in Otto's direction to say goodbye, then raises his voice slightly to call to Harry to stop. Harry either can't hear him or is just ignoring him and continues his slow pace.

Ivy chats with Otto for a moment before yet another dog comes into the park and Otto heads over to film it, Hildy casually following him at a distance.

Ivy and Toby continue their walk and return home about half an hour later. Ivy sits at her desk, and before getting back to work, she thinks of Jason and how nice and rare it is to have a good interaction with a stranger, even at the best of times, let alone now.

If truth be told, Ivy did know that Jason lived in her building. She didn't recognize him at first, with his mask on, and with his hair longer. But she once saw Jason in the lobby of their building, apprehensively but politely chatting with Annie, the overly-friendly woman who lives in the apartment below Ivy's.

She remembered it because she felt bad for Jason at the time, having experienced being trapped by Annie's forced conversation before. Ivy could tell he was looking for a way to leave and it had occurred to her that she could save him by distracting Annie with some inane question or a comment about someone not properly separating their recycling so Jason could make his escape, but Ivy had been running late for an appointment and didn't have time to save a stranger.

Then, a few days after that incident, Annie cornered Ivy in her well-intentioned but socially unaware way and confessed that she suspected Jason had a sad past. "He just has a kind of melancholy behind his eyes, you know?" Annie had said.

But from their brief interaction today, Jason certainly didn't seem melancholy. Or not more than anyone else seems right now. Ivy wonders if maybe Annie was just picking up on Jason's desire to get away from the obligatory conversation, something Ivy could definitely relate to.

CHAPTER 5

"I think if we go back and click on the book spines, those might be clues," Ivy says into her computer's microphone.

"I tried those and nothing came up, but I'll try again," Anthony replies.

"Maybe go slower," Dustin chimes in.

"That's what *she* said," Ivy adds.

Thanks to the pandemic, virtual escape rooms have become a thing! And Ivy, Anthony, and Anthony's husband, Dustin, are in one, trying to gather clues from the haunted house's library. Only three more rooms to go before they can banish the demons that possess this house back to hell and win the feeling of superiority you get from beating an escape room. Virtual or otherwise.

About an hour later, they solve the puzzle and "escape" with plenty of time to spare. Dustin leaves to feed the dogs and Anthony stays on a bit with Ivy, just to chat.

Anthony closes the door to the office and returns to his computer leaning into the camera for dramatic effect to stage whisper, "My husband is not handling isolation well."

Ivy whispers back, conspiratorially, scooting closer to her camera as well. "What is he doing?"

"He's started smoking again. But he thinks he's hiding it from me. He's probably outside smoking right now."

"That's a smelly habit to try to hide."

"It is. And he thinks we should do every home project we ever thought of doing. Which, is the most productive way to spend our time and probably what we *should* do, but it's not how I *want* to spend my time."

"What kind of shit are we talking about? Like deep cleaning or like repairs or decorating?"

"All of the above! I talked him out of building a guest house himself, but we'll soon have a greenhouse. And he's found all the supplies online. Apparently, when the shit hits the fan, most people do not decide it's time to do some home reno. They tend to try to cover basic needs, like food and toilet paper. Hence those supply shortages. But Dustin is not most people, so those special project supplies are all in stock. Nobody else wants them now!" Anthony replies, keeping his voice down and his face close to the camera.

"I see a lot of sorting through stuff in the closets in your future," Ivy replies.

"It's already begun."

Anthony and Ivy continue to chat until they get a notice that their time is about to run out. The two make plans to try the Disney+ Groupwatch feature as another fun new way to socialize safely. Ivy closes her laptop and notices Toby staring at her. She checks her watch and sees it is indeed already time for his before bed walk. Ivy looks back at Toby with a smile.

"Damn dude, your internal clock is spot on!"

Toby wags his tail in reply.

When they get back home, Ivy decides to do laundry, still hyped from the novelty of the escape room and interacting with other humans, albeit virtually. At this time of night, she should have the machines all to herself.

How she longs for a day when she can have her own washer and dryer *inside* her own home. What a luxury. The laundry room she has planned for her mansion is pretty amazing. But for now, it's the communal basement laundry room for her!

Ivy jams two loads' worth of clothes and her laundry supplies into her big blue IKEA shopping bag, puts on her mask, and heads downstairs.

As she walks in, she's surprised to see Jason there, cleaning the buttons of the dryer with an antibacterial wipe.

"Oh, hi," Ivy says.

"Hi," he replies. "Give me one minute and the washers are all yours."

"No rush." Ivy says crossing the fluorescent-lit room and setting down her giant bag of clothes on the folding table to avoid the awkwardness of just watching him.

"Where did you get cleaning wipes? I haven't been able to find them anywhere," Ivy says, mostly to fill the silence.

"Oh, I always have these," Jason says. "I'm one of those paranoid weirdos who already had hand sanitizer, wipes, gloves, and masks in bulk."

Ivy then notices he is indeed wearing gloves. And two masks. Not knowing what to say next, Ivy just nods in a way that she hopes conveys something along the lines of, "Oh, cool," and then she pretends to have very important texts that need her immediate attention.

As she mindlessly scrolls through Instagram, she mentally congratulates herself that she didn't wash her makeup off before coming down here. Since working from home, she puts the effort into her appearance only when she feels like it. Something she's decided will continue when she has to return to the office. Screw trying to impress others. But … if she *happens* to look her best for this guy who she found charming, that's a nice bonus.

Is she maybe sucking in her gut and maintaining her best posture when she hears Jason's voice say, "All clear." Yes. Shut up.

"Thank you," Ivy says as she smiles at him knowing full-well he can't see it. She loads the washer as she obsesses over this brief interaction, stressing that she somehow came off as a freak. Maybe she should have just left and done laundry another time? Would that have been less weird in any way? Probably running out of the room would have actually looked crazy.

When Ivy returns to the laundry room later to switch over her clothes, she finds a note on the washer.

Hi,

Sorry! I think the dryers might be broken again, my clothes weren't dry and I needed to put them in for more time. Here's my number. If you're comfortable with it, text me your number and I'll text you when my clothes are out of the dryer so you don't have to keep checking back.

555-747-1123.

Jason

Ivy smiles and takes the note back up to her apartment with her where she enters Jason's number into her phone and texts.

IVY

This is Ivy, thanks for the note.

JASON
Sorry about this.
I hope the extra fifteen minutes will be
enough, but I'll text you when I'm done with
the dryer

IVY
No problem

JASON
<poop emoji>
Sorry!
I meant to hit the <grimacing emoji>

IVY
I thought you were warning me that you
shat in the dryer

Ivy hits send and then immediately regrets having done so, feeling
it might be too crass too soon, but Jason replies after a short pause.

JASON
Haha, no. Not this time at least.
<winking emoji>

About twenty minutes later, Ivy receives a text from Jason letting her
know the dryer is hers. Though, logically, she knows that he shouldn't still
be down there, she takes a moment to spray a little volumizing dry
shampoo in her hair and make sure her eye make-up hasn't relocated to
under her eyes (for her own self-esteem, certainly not to impress him) and
when she goes down to put her clothes in the dryer, Jason is there.

"Sorry!" Jason says, "I realized I forgot to clean the lint trap, so I had
to come back down. I couldn't have you thinking I was *that* guy."

"Oh yah, I would have judged you. Harshly," Ivy replies, as Jason
throws the lint into the trash.

"Well, good night," Jason says as he leaves the room.

"You too!"

Ivy takes a moment to subtly check Jason out as he leaves. Not bad. He has broad shoulders and a toned back and though she's not really an ass lady, he does have a good butt. And his hair, damn! So full and shiny. She imagines running her fingers through it. Then she imagines him running his fingers through *her* hair and maybe tugging it a little, like while he leans her head back- no! She is taking a break from men. Yes, a much-needed break from all men, even the charming and cute ones.

CHAPTER 6

Ivy surveys her apartment with a critical eye.

The first month of quarantine, she was adjusting to being home and figuring out where her work files should go as well as just lacking any motivation to organize things. As a result, there were often stacks of mail she did not want to deal with, piles of laundry she needed to fold and put away, dishes in the sink, and rotting food in the fridge.

But now, the nesting phase has kicked in. Faced with being trapped in her home, suddenly her number one goal is making it as inviting as possible, and that meant a lot of cleaning. No more walking into the kitchen and thinking, "I should break down those boxes and take them downstairs," only to leave them and have the same thought the next ten times she walked into the kitchen.

So, when Ivy sees she left a couple of dishes languishing in the sink, she knows they have sat there long enough and must be dealt with now. She puts in her earbuds, turns on a podcast, slides on her dish gloves and is ready to get down to business.

But as she turns on the faucet, the water sputters, and the stream is weak for a moment until it dies out completely. Ivy tries the bathroom sink and finds the same problem. She curses the building manager, Mike, who probably just shut off the water for some reason without giving any notice. Who does that when everyone is stuck indoors? Ivy thinks fondly of the last building manager, she always seemed on top of things.

Then, never letting an opportunity to chastise herself go by, she thinks of how if she just owned her own home, this wouldn't be an issue. Why hasn't she made better life choices? Then, she has the irrational thought that maybe it's just *her* apartment having issues. It's unlikely, there's certainly no reason for it to be true, but now, unfortunately, the thought is in her head. After a brief hesitation, she grabs her phone. It couldn't hurt to just check in with Jason, right? Just to make sure it's a building issue, not a *her* issue.

> IVY
> Sorry to bother you, but is your water out?
> (This is Ivy, ground floor flunky)

She stops herself from writing "You know, the woman with the huge tits and the ass that won't quit" and is very happy she refrained when there is not an immediate response. If she had dared to send that little joke and it was met with silence, she would have fallen down a hole of regret she wouldn't have been able to escape the rest of the night.

Ivy puts down the phone in an attempt to just forget about what she's done and looks around for another chore to complete. As she begins to sweep her kitchen, she hears her text alert.

JASON
Now that you mention it, yes.
Hadn't noticed

> IVY
> Ok, thanks
> Just wanted to make sure it wasn't just me.

JASON
Mike probably shut it off without telling
anyone

> IVY
> That's what I figured but thought I'd
> double check
> Thanks! Sorry to bother you

JASON
No problem

While Ivy is relieved to know nothing is specifically wrong with her plumbing, she also knows she will now spend some part of the night overthinking whether she should have 'bugged' Jason or not. Maybe using his number like that was crossing a line? Did she just violate the sacred social contract of laundry room buddies? Did she weaken the bond of good neighbors? Had she really expected him to reply, "My water is out and oh, by the way, I really felt a connection with you, did you feel it too? Come over to my place and we can we enjoy not having water together and then fall in love."

Ultimately, Ivy distracts herself with a podcast in her earbuds and The Office on in the background and gets back to tidying.

CHAPTER 7

The next day, Ivy and Toby head down to the park where they see Otto following Harry with his camera as Jason keeps an extra safe distance, obviously trying not to be included in the shot. Ivy wonders how the hell she went from never seeing this guy from her building to seeing him three times in one week.

"Toby!" Otto shouts as soon as he spots them. Toby walks straight over to Harry and greets him with excited whining and sniffing. "That's going to be a great video," Otto says as he maneuvers the camera to capture different angles of the interaction.

"He's going to need an agent soon," Jason says to Ivy, as he comes a little closer, while still allowing more than six feet between them. "He's really cute."

"Aw, thanks, but I don't want to be one of those stage moms," Ivy says.

"Toby really is great on camera. You can tell that Harry likes him too," Otto says and Ivy laughs because Harry could not look more indifferent.

"He doesn't have a lot of energy," Jason says, referring to Harry, "But I swear, he is enjoying himself."

"I'm glad. Toby doesn't really get this excited with many dogs," Ivy says.

"You two should take them out together. It would be good for them," Otto suggests, a little mischievous twinkle in his eye.

Ivy glances at Jason who takes his eyes off the flirting dogs and looks up at her, both knowing exactly what Otto is up to.

"Well, we walk four times a day," Ivy offers. "You guys are welcome to join if you'd like."

"Four times?" Jason says, more in awe than in judgement. "Wow, Toby is lucky. Harry isn't much of a walker anymore, maybe we'll join you guys for *one* of those."

Ivy feels herself blush and is, for the first time, glad she has to wear a mask.

Ivy and Toby walk down the hallway, passing package after package left in front of apartment doors. Turns out, during a pandemic, people who do not have to walk a dog several times a day and who now don't even need to leave their homes to go to work, do not always know when they have packages waiting for them. It's not uncommon for a box or large envelope to sit in the hall for a day or so. Or perhaps the recipients know but are still letting their packages decontaminate in the hall rather than in their homes. Whatever the reason, the hall now frequently has a lot of labels for Ivy to peek at.

The difference with the box outside apartment one, the unit closest to the building's main door, is that it has been sitting in the hall for *several* days. Of course, the first time Ivy passed it, she noticed the company and, not recognizing the name, thought nothing of it. Nice Lady is probably a germophobe and isn't leaving her apartment right now, no big deal. But the package sits there long enough that there seems to be a smell radiating from it.

On the third day it sits in the hall, Ivy happens to see a commercial for the company advertised on the box. It's a food delivery service, which could explain the smell, but Ivy knows immediately, from some little back corner of her brain, that something is wrong. It's possible to not realize you have a random package outside your door, an impulse-buy that maybe you forgot was coming, but food delivery would be expected. You would know it was there.

Ivy decides if the box is still here on their pre-bed walk, she will do some investigating. Sure enough, the box is still there and Ivy notices that the smell, which has gotten quite potent, does not seem to be coming from the box. Or not just the box. As she steps outside, the smell is actually worse and that's when Ivy notices that the window to apartment one is open. The rotting stench is coming from inside the apartment.

Toby is determined to continue their walk, not aware that Ivy is in the middle of something. As they walk, Ivy pulls out her phone to call Mike. He, of course, doesn't answer, but his wife does. Ivy explains that she has noticed a package outside of apartment one's door for a few days now and there's a smell coming from the apartment. She's hoping that just this information will be enough for the woman to put two and two together so she can avoid actually articulating her full concern.

Unfortunately, Mrs. Mike is not able to add those facts up and tells Ivy that her gout is acting up so she can't come get the package, but if Ivy wants, she can bring it up to their door and she'll have Mike deal with it tomorrow.

Ivy tries one more time to explain without just blurting out, "The lady in apartment one is dead!" She takes a breath. "I don't think it's the package itself. I'm concerned for the woman *in* the apartment because when I stepped outside, the smell was worse, and her window is open."

After a significant pause, Mrs. Mike finally understands and immediately begins to cry. "I know she's had some health problems, but I hope she's okay. She's so nice."

Mrs. Mike lets Ivy go telling her that she will call the police for a wellness check since she cannot go down there to check herself and Mike, the actual building manager, the person whose responsibility this should be, the man who has definitely passed that same package as many times as Ivy but didn't do anything about it, won't be home for a while.

A few minutes after Ivy and Toby return home from their walk, she sees the lights of an emergency vehicle outside the building and peeks her head into the hall to see a uniformed fireman knocking on Nice Lady's door. There is no answer, and the lights are still flashing outside her window two hours later when Ivy eventually falls asleep.

When they pass the door on their way out for their morning walk the next day, Ivy sees that there is a Coroner's Office sticker sealing the door closed and her eyes fill with tears.

As she watched Toby sniff and pee and have a great time, Ivy's nose is running inside her mask. While it is, of course, sad a person has died, Ivy isn't sure why she is *this* upset. Is it partly the isolation she herself feels? Maybe it's simply the fact that nobody noticed Nice Lady had died. Whatever the reason, Ivy calls in sick that day, unable to focus on her work.

When Jason texts about joining them on their walk, Ivy considers ignoring the message. Or maybe responding but pretending her calendar is crazy for the next few days; she just doesn't feel like being around people at the moment. But she decides it might be good to socialize. Also, she will actually need to walk Toby. Lying to someone who lives in your building is tricky. So, she invites Jason to join them on tomorrow's long morning walk. They agree to meet outside at 10AM.

CHAPTER 8

Toby and Ivy are already waiting out front of the building as Jason and Harry step outside. Jason appears to be wearing a backpack and Ivy has a moment of concern that he was expecting a lot more out of this walk than what she and Toby usually do. Their walks do not require supplies.

"Sorry to keep you waiting," Jason says. "He wanted to walk, so I let him but then he was extra slow and each time I bent down to pick him up, he'd pick up the pace again."

"That's Okay," Ivy replies. "Toby has been sniffing this bush for the last couple of minutes, so we weren't going anywhere anyway. Where do you guys normally walk? How far can Harry go?"

"Oh, don't worry about him, I've got him covered," Jason says as he turns around to show her that the thing on his back is a dog carrier, not a backpack. "I'll be carrying him most of the way."

"Like Jesus in the sand," Ivy replies, before she can stop herself.

"Exactly," Jason says with a chuckle.

They are all quiet for a moment as Jason and Ivy watch the dogs obsessively sniff, uninterested in going anywhere. Jason fills the void by asking, "Did you see the sirens the other night? I hope everyone was okay."

Ivy stiffens a bit and decides not to feign ignorance. "The woman in apartment one died."

"Oh, that's too bad. Did you know her?" Jason asks cautiously.

"Not really. She once told me Toby was quiet and cute, so I liked her. But that was about it."

"That's sad," Jason offers, but while Ivy has not been outright cold in her responses, he gets the feeling she doesn't want to discuss this, so he doesn't say anything else on the subject.

After a bit more sniffing and a little coaxing from Ivy, Toby begins walking in his usual happy trot and, seeing his pace, Jason scoops Harry up into his arms and places him in the pack, which he leaves on his chest making it more of a standard baby carrier.

Forcing a chipper tone to make up for her inability to make polite conversation, Ivy says, "I never know how much actual walking versus how much sniffing Toby will want to do. Usually, for the first ten minutes of our walks, we can't go more than two feet before some scent distracts him and he stops to investigate. It figures that today with Harry, he's extra peppy."

"It's okay," says Jason. "We just needed to get out of the apartment. I normally carry Harry outside, he stands for a moment, pees and/or poops, then we go back in and he goes back to sleep. That's the only fresh air we get."

Ivy glances at Harry who has indeed already fallen asleep with his head on Jason's chest. Ivy smiles at how peaceful he looks and then has a terrible thought that Harry might actually be dead. Jason reads her mind.

"It's Okay, he's just sleeping. I can hear him breathing," he says, the crinkles around his eyes indicating a smile under his mask.

"Oh good. That would have been a terrible beginning to our journey," Ivy says jokingly and immediately hopes she did not offend him. But Jason seems to take it in the way it was intended, which she considers a good sign since sarcastic flippancy is her standard. His acceptance makes her happy she agreed to this walk and allows her to loosen up a little.

Jason and Ivy chitchat amiably as they walk as far apart as the sidewalks will allow, Jason often walking into the street or grass whenever possible to increase the distance.

Their conversation comes around to Harry Potter, and Jason mentions that Harry, who is still asleep on his chest, is named after the titular character. Ivy does her best not to swoon learning that Jason is a fan of the series.

"Toby is a rescue and he came with that name, but if I had been in charge of naming him, I probably would have used a Harry Potter name. Possibly Collin Creevy. Maybe Seamus, just because I like the name. I don't know, Dobby is a little too on the nose since Toby has those giant ears." She pauses to take a breath. "Did I just reveal too much Harry Potter knowledge for a forty-year-old woman?"

Smiling, Jason replies, "Well, I followed all of that, so if you know too much, so do I. I'm actually more surprised that you're forty. I would have guessed early thirties."

Ivy stops walking and faces Jason, "Marry me."

Jason laughs. "Oh you don't want that. Believe me. Just ask my ex."

"Uh oh. What would she . . ." and Ivy pauses for Jason to confirm that his ex was, in fact, a woman. He nods in confirmation and Ivy continues. "What would she say about you?"

"Where would she even begin? I work too hard, I care too much, I love Harry Potter too much," Jason says dryly while giving Ivy a smile and a side glance.

"No such thing! She clearly had strong Dursley vibes," Ivy says in mock outrage.

"A total Petunia," he agrees.

Ivy is enjoying Jason's company so much that she takes them on the longest of her pre-approved routes and they enjoy light and steady conversation. Unavoidably, much of their talk is about the pandemic. They discuss their frustrations and stresses and detail their new daily quarantine routines, which they decide to call quaroutines.

"I have established a sort of quarantine zone around my front door," Jason explains. "I've always left my shoes at the door, but now I leave anything that went outside there. Nothing leaves the zone until I properly sanitize it. I even leave mail and other packages there, I spray them down with Lysol and then let them sit for 24 hours. Aside from these walks, I basically don't leave my apartment."

"What are you doing about groceries?" Ivy asks.

He replies with light sarcasm. "Let me tell you, it's a real treat. I've mostly been living off canned foods and frozen foods. A pandemic is like my worst nightmare, so the first I heard of a real-life plague coming our way, I stocked up. I have a ton of non-perishables."

"That sounds . . . yummy?"

"Oh, it's terrible. I'm so fucking sick of beans, tuna, soup, and Lean Cuisines. I would love to go to the store, but I'm avoiding public spaces until this shit blows over." Jason says.

"I don't want to be a downer, but I think we're going to be in this shit for the rest of the year," Ivy replies regretfully.

"Oh god, please don't say that."

"I don't *want* that to be the case. But I'm not optimistic. That being said, I go to the store about once a week. So, if you need me to pick some things up for you, let me know. Maybe some *fresh* vegetables? *Fresh* fruit?" Ivy says, trying to tempt him.

"Vegetables that don't require a can opener? Sounds fancy," Jason says.

"Oh it is! Pure luxury."

"Thank you for the offer," he says, genuinely. "It is tempting. I'll keep it in mind,"

On their way back home, about half a block from their building, Jason takes Harry out of his carrier and places him gently on the ground to give him an opportunity to stretch his legs. They watch as Harry totters in front of them, slowly but surely making his way home.

Toby notices that Harry has been set free and decides his sniffing can wait, determined to lead the way. Toby pulls ahead of all of them, stopping to sniff only long enough that Harry can't pass him.

"It's not a race, Toby," Ivy says as she and Jason watch the two dogs in a comfortable silence. Both dogs become distracted by a spot of yellowing grass that needs investigating and as they sniff intently, Jason looks at Ivy.

"Fuck, marry, kill. Harry, Ron, Hermione. Go." Jason says.

"Oooo. I honestly can't believe I haven't thought about this before. Ummmm. This is tough but I'm going to marry Harry, fuck Hermione, and kill Ron."

"Interesting," Jason says.

"Hermione is a bit of a nag, so I don't want to be married to her. And I like Ron and all, but he offers the least to society. So, my choices are also for the greater good."

"I would have chosen the same. Harry would be a good partner."

"He really would!" Ivy says with sincere bonhomie.

When they reach their apartment building, Ivy and Jason manage to enter the building while maintaining a safe distance before they pause at the stairs leading up to Jason's floor.

"That was fun," Jason says. "Maybe Harry and I can join you guys again soon?"

"Of course," Ivy replies. "We usually walk around the same time every day. Toby loves a strict schedule."

"Works for us. It'll be good for me to get into the habit of getting up before noon."

"Well, if you're feeling super ambitious, you're welcome to join us for our early morning walk, it's usually around 5:30 or 6:00am. Interested?" Ivy teases.

"That's messed up," Jason says.

"I know, I'm one of those insufferable morning people. So, you're joining us for out 10AM walk tomorrow??"

"Yah, that'd be great."

"Good. See you guys tomorrow," Ivy says, with a wave as she and Toby head down the hall. Ivy smiles to herself, feeling content from a long overdue quality human interaction.

The next day, Jason sends her a text apologizing that he will not be able to make their walk today as planned. He adds that he is hoping he can join her and Toby soon. Just probably not this week, but doesn't elaborate on why he's cancelling. Ivy has a pang of disappointment but doesn't dwell on it.

IVY
No problem, you're welcome any time

Jason receives her friendly reply and feels even worse about cancelling. The truth is, he has no real reason not to go. He just couldn't deal with being a human today. He woke up in a shitty mood and doesn't want to talk to anyone. He doesn't want to feel anything, even if it's a positive feeling.

Jason found Ivy to be very easy to talk to and a very good listener. He had a nice time on their walk. He knows there is no logical reason not to want to experience that again, but something is holding him back.

He has a feeling that if he just told her he wasn't in the mood to socialize, she would probably understand, but he represses that urge to be honest with her. He's not ready to risk sharing possibly uncomfortable truths quite yet.

Instead, he plants himself on his couch, turns on the TV, and spends the rest of the day watching whatever Netflix has to offer. He doesn't even remember most of what he watches, it's just background noise as he plays games on his phone. The only breaks he takes are to carry Harry outside, which he has intentionally timed at odd hours of the day, so he doesn't risk running into anyone.

Ivy is not so lucky.

As she and Toby make their way outside, she hears someone call her name from the lobby. She doesn't even need to see who it is to know that it's chatty Annie. Nobody else would try to talk to her.

Ivy takes a fraction of a second to decide she can't realistically claim to have not heard Annie. Then she takes another second to curse herself for wearing her left earbud today and not her right. If she had the right one in, it would be facing the lobby and she definitely could have pretended she didn't hear anything. Or hell, she actually might not have heard Annie's chipper voice call out to her.

But, Ivy made her choices and now she must live with them.

This is one of the many reasons she needs her own house with her own yard. And a privacy fence. And tall bushes. Anything to avoid forced conversations with neighbors.

"Hi Annie," Ivy says as she stops where she is rather than walking into the lobby to get closer. "How have you been?"

Annie closes her mailbox and takes a few steps toward Ivy, but maintains a safe distance. Annie causally flips through the envelopes in her hands, not looking at Ivy, almost as though Ivy has interrupted her, not the other way around.

"Oh I'm hanging in there," Annie says, "How are you?"

"I'm Okay. Toby and I were just heading out for some fresh air," Ivy replies, dropping a subtle hint to Annie that she *was* going somewhere and would like to get back to it.

"Toby is so cute," Annie says as she bends down to make eye contact with him. As she does so, her long flowing skirt touches the floor and her necklaces hang forward. Ivy's always been fascinated by Annie's fashion sense; she dresses somewhere between a Renaissance Fair employee and a hippie. It's a look Ivy can't quite put her finger on. But even now, Annie has obviously carefully put together her ensemble.

"Did you hear about Susan?" Annie asks, clearly getting ready to gossip.

"Susan?" Ivy replies, going through a mental rolodex trying to work out who the hell Susan is and why Annie would expect her to know Susan.

"Susan lived in apartment one. So sad, she passed away. They don't think it was COVID. It appears to be natural causes. No foul play. She was only in her sixties, should have had plenty of years ahead of her."

"That is sad," Ivy confirms. "I didn't know her name, but she seemed nice."

"I've been in this neighborhood so long, I know everybody," Annie brags. And then with a somewhat abrupt change of subject, she continues, "I saw you and Toby walking with Jason and Harry. I'm so happy you two found each other. It's nice to have company, especially at a time like this."

Ivy can't help but be a little impressed with Annie's awareness of everyone and everything in the neighborhood. Ivy enjoys trying to see what her neighbors order or what their names are, but she's got nothing on Annie who really does know everybody. And not just their names, but their spouse's, kids' and pets' names as well. And probably their siblings' and parents' names and maybe their favorite colors.

Sometimes, when Annie has forced Ivy to chat with her, Annie will just start dropping names, clearly assuming Ivy also knows everyone in the neighborhood. Ivy rarely has any clue who she's talking about. When Ivy was new to the building, she would ask Annie who these people were, but she soon realized she'd never remember all of them and learned to just nod when Annie shares neighborhood updates.

"It is nice to have company," Ivy agrees. She can't think of anything else to say, but that's not a problem for Annie.

"I told Shalene she should ask Jason out but then she met Brett and you know how that's going."

Ivy doesn't know who Shalene and Brett are and, therefore, has no way of knowing how it's going, so she just nods.

"I'm surprised Jason is even leaving his apartment; he's so scared of germs. But I'm glad he is, he's such a nice guy. It's good he's making connections," Annie concludes.

"He is nice." Ivy's main strategy with Annie is to just agree with her, answer any direct questions as succinctly as possible, then get the hell out.

"How long have you two been seeing each other?" Annie asks, a slight raise to her eyebrows, clearly entering information gathering mode.

"Well, we're not *seeing* each other," Ivy clarifies. "Otto introduced us at the park and suggested Toby and Harry walk together."

"Otto loves to bring people together," Annie says with a slightly snarky tone.

Now *this* is the gossip Ivy wants to hear about. She's long wondered what is up with Annie and Otto. Otto mentioned Annie once, but with no hint of any serious history or any bad blood, just in passing. But any time Annie talks about Otto, there is definitely something there.

It's certainly possible the two were lovers, but Ivy likes to pretend Annie and Otto stopped to talk at some point and Annie became enraged when she realized Otto is the only person on the planet who can out-talk her. Perhaps they stood for hours just chatting until Annie gave up and went home in a rage vowing to never speak to him again.

"Well, Toby and I should get going," Ivy says as Toby conveniently moves toward the door.

Ignoring this, Annie says, "I'm sure you know this, but Jason was in the middle of a divorce when he moved here. It's been finalized for a while. And I haven't seen any women going in and out of his place, so I think it's about time for him to move on."

Ivy smiles knowing that there was no way Jason just offered that information on his own. How does Annie get secrets out of people? It's probably that she's just bold enough to ask the uncomfortable questions that polite social skills would prevent most people from asking.

Ivy can't even imagine questioning someone she passed in the hall in such an intrusive manner. "So, you married? Oh, single huh? Never found the right one? Divorced! What a shame! What happened? Tell me everything!"

It's almost admirable. If you ignore how rude it is.

"I'll let you two go," Annie says, but then follows that with, "Are you working from home now?"

So close to escaping. "Yes, I have to go in occasionally, but for the most part, I'm at home. Which is nice. Toby is really enjoying me being home," Ivy adds, to appear like she's making an effort in this conversation.

"Jason works from home too, doesn't he?" Annie asks.

"Actually, I don't know. We didn't discuss that on our one walk," she replies, hoping Annie picked up on the "one".

"I think he does. I think he works with computers or software or something like that. Something an old bitty like me wouldn't understand."

Ivy always finds it funny that Annie acts like she's ancient or enfeebled. If Ivy had to guess, she'd say Annie was sixty, tops. Maybe Annie has learned that people will tolerate you longer and share more with you if they see you as a wizened old grandmother.

"Yah, I don't know what he does," Ivy says. And then, making it clear she's really done this time, she and Toby head outside as she gives Annie a parting, "We've got to go, have a good day."

CHAPTER 9

After a week of his self-imposed solitude, Jason is ready to risk human interaction again. It's funny, he didn't used to be like this. His whole life, Jason was very friendly and outgoing. The type of person who was comfortable going to a party alone because he knew he'd make a friend. Not that he went to many parties alone as a married man, but if Nicole was busy or just didn't feel like going out, he was fine with that too.

Now, however, he often finds there are just stretches of time where he's happy to be alone and the thought of having to put on a happy face is exhausting. But he also knows that if he stays isolated too long, his family gets worried. So, his first call is to his mom, whom he should have called a few days ago.

His mother and stepfather moved to Palm Springs a few years back, which is closer than they used to be, but still far enough that he doesn't see them as much as he really should. He's usually good about calling regularly though. Enough to stay in touch.

"Good morning, honey," his mom, Margaret, says. Her faded Boston accent and maternal tone immediately reminding Jason of home while simultaneously making him feel guilty for putting off the call for so long.

"Hi Mom, how are you?"

"Oh, we're just fine. How are you?"

"Fine."

"How's Harry?"

"He's fine," Jason replies, glancing over at Harry curled up in his bed, halfway burrowed under a blanket. "He's hanging in there."

His mom proceeds to update him on all her local friends, none of whom he has never met, and how each of them is dealing with the pandemic. As they wrap up the call, his mom's tone changes, and he knows she's about to start her interrogation.

"Have you heard from Nicole?" she asks.

"What? No, mom. Why would I have?"

"I don't know. It must be hard not talking to her; you were together for so long. Don't you think it would be nice to catch up?"

"We have nothing to say to each other," Jason says, his tone having gotten cold.

"Honey, hasn't it been long enough? I know she would like to talk to you."

"Wait, have you been talking to her?" Jason asks.

"Yes," Margaret confesses.

"For how long?"

She chooses to ignore this question. "I know she made a mistake, but she was a part of all our lives for over twenty years. I still remember what you both wore to prom for god's sake. She was like a daughter to me, that doesn't just go away."

"Sure, but I'm your actual son. And your cherished *daughter* broke my goddamn heart, so I would sort of think you wouldn't want to treat her like family anymore," Jason says, surprising himself with his hostility.

Margaret pauses a moment. "Jason, do you really want me to stop talking to Nicole?" she asks, sincerely.

Jason takes a deep breath and regroups before answering. "No, you can talk to her if you want to. Just don't expect me to talk to her."

"Honey, I don't want you-" she starts, but Jason cuts her off.

"I'm going to go now. Good night." He ends the call and returns to the TV, turning on some docuseries at random. Anything to distract him.

After he's calmed down a bit, he texts Ivy.

Ivy is on her bed, not quite in the fetal position but damn close. As she waits for her grocery store brand pain reliever to kick in, she tries some deep breathing to see if it helps the cramping. It doesn't. She has a fleeting memory of having gotten one of those microwavable heating pads for Christmas last year, a cute sloth, but can't remember where she put it. While she begins to mentally chastise herself for her disorganization, her phone dings.

JASON
Harry and I would like to join you guys for a
walk Does today work for you?

> IVY
> I would love for you guys to join us
> again, but I don't feel well today. Maybe
> tomorrow?

There's a slight delay in response. Nothing crazy, but enough to make Ivy realize she should clarify her illness.

> IVY
> Don't worry, it's not Corona
> Just girly cramps

JASON
Glad to hear it
(That it's not COVID)
Not glad to hear you have cramps
I was trying not to panic while deciding how I
would delicately ask if you had a deadly and
super contagious disease
That's not something I ever thought I'd need
consider the etiquette for

IVY
Yah, I just realized that I can't get away
with vague texts like that right now
I guess for future reference, I will
specifically warn you if I'm having
COVID symptoms
"Not feeling well" probably means girly
issues or diarrhea. Maybe both!
You're regretting texting me, aren't
you?

JASON
No <smiley face emoji>
I'm glad we're setting this precedent
I get diarrhea too, you know. I might need this
code as well.
Can I bring you anything?

Ivy smiles at this. While she appreciates the offer, there's no way in
hell she would ever ask a man to help her with problems like this. It's too

personal and vulnerable. Plus, men can't usually handle the details of menstruation and she doesn't like the idea of Jason thinking of her as icky.

> IVY
> No, thank you
> That's very sweet of you to ask though

JASON
Let me know if you change your mind
I don't want to brag, but I make amazing
brownies
They may not completely get rid of your
cramps, but they might distract you enough
that the cramps will be weakened

> IVY
> OMG! Cramp kryptonite?

JASON
Basically

> IVY
> Are you an angel sent directly from
> Heaven?

JASON
Yes
Please don't tell anyone

IVY
Your secret is safe with me
Just looking up the LA Times tip line
Unrelated though

JASON
Thank you for your discretion

IVY
I will keep the brownies in mind, if
things get REALLY bad I'll let you know
The drugs should be kicking in soon
though

JASON
Ok. Feel better

Ivy, still smiling and feeling mildly less like death, rolls over to take a little nap. Which turns into a big nap. When she wakes up a few hours later, she's feeling much better. When she checks her phone, she sees she has a text from Jason.

JASON
I didn't want to knock and upset Toby and
disturb you, but I left some fresh brownies
outside your door. Even if you don't want them
now, it's never a bad idea to have brownies on
hand. I wore a mask while I made them and I
keep a clean kitchen, they should be safe.

Ivy goes to her door, looks through the peephole to make sure the coast is clear, and retrieves a paper grocery bag from in front of her door. There are five brownies inside, each packaged in their own sandwich bag. She opens one and takes a bite. They're still warm and the chocolate chips inside are all melty. She swoons a little from the warm chocolatey goodness. She can't help but moan.

Grabbing her phone, Ivy eagerly types a message to. She considers sending just the word "brownie" followed by the squirting water drops and a taco emoji. But decides that might be inappropriate, even if it's accurate.

> IVY
> Just woke up. THANK YOU. That was so thoughtful. These brownies are amazing

Jason replies after a brief pause, clearly close to his phone.

JASON
You're welcome
Hope they help

> IVY
> I hope you didn't have to go to the store for the ingredients

JASON
For you, I would have
<winking emoji>
But I did have the ingredients on hand
Like a real mother fucking baker

IVY
I love that you have been living off
canned goods for weeks but have all
the ingredients for brownies
It's good to see your priorities are in
order
I approve

JASON
I make good choices

IVY
Well, thank you again
I'm sure these will cure me
Do you want to join me and Toby for our
walk tomorrow?

JASON
Yes
See you guys then

And at 10am the next day, they start their journey.

"My new favorite thing to do," Ivy explains to Jason, "is to open all my windows as soon as soon as I log off work, then I select the fireplace thing on Netflix and sit in front of my TV, under a blanket, playing Plants vs Zombies, while listening to an audiobook."

"What's the fireplace thing?" Jason asks, intrigued.

"It's on Netflix, so I guess it would be considered a show? I don't know what you'd call it. But there are a couple of ambient backgrounds where you just watch some logs burn in a fireplace and listen to the crackling wood. It's very calming."

"Huh, I will have to check that out. I've been watching documentaries and then when they're done, I realize I haven't retained any of the information," Jason confesses.

"Yah, I have to be in the right mood to handle new information right now. When I do watch something, not just have it on in the background, I've been bingeing things I've already seen a million times like The Office," Ivy says.

"British or American?"

"American." She continues somewhat hesitantly, "Don't judge me, but I don't like the British Office."

"What? I don't think I've ever heard anyone say that," Jason says with faux outrage.

"I know! I *appreciate* a lot of British comedies, but I don't actually enjoy watching them."

"This is shocking information," Jason says. "I don't know if we can be friends. Monty Python blew my mind as a kid."

"I know that I'm in the minority here, but it's just how I feel. And you know what else? British autobiographies are boring. There, I've said it," Ivy states defiantly.

"Wait, what? That's a very broad claim. That can't be true."

"It is true. I have listened to a bunch. And autobiographies are usually great to listen to because the author reads it, and you really get a good feel for their personality. But for whatever reason, when British celebrities decide to share their stories, it is mind-numbingly boring."

"Now that you mention it, I guess I don't really read biographies, so I can't really argue," Jason says.

"Even for people with interesting lives," Ivy continues, becoming more animated she explains. "They're boring! I first noticed it with Sharon Osbourne's book, which I did read as opposed to listen to, it's possible that hearing her would have made it better. But she has had a crazy life and still, boring. I think maybe it's the old British stiff upper lip or something. Everything is so subdued. The only exception I've found is Simon Pegg's autobiography and that's probably only because every other chapter is a fictional story where he's a spy or something."

"Well, it's good to know that you hate the British."

"I don't! I swear!"

"I'm telling the queen!" Jason declares.

"Noooo! She'll take back my tiara!"

"Diadem, please," he replies.

"I'm so sorry, you're right," Ivy smiles at the Harry Potter allusion.

"Well, if we're confessing personal biases, I should probably tell you that I wholeheartedly believe people who voluntarily wake up before the sun aren't right in the head," he teases.

"Wait a damn min—"

"Yah, now you know how those poor British celebrities feel!"

CHAPTER 10

Ivy lies sprawled out across her bed, sunken into its excessive pillows and blankets, talking to her sister, Holly, on the phone. Because they live in different states, the two have established a tradition of watching Great British Baking Show together every Friday night to make sure to stay in touch.

But since the new season hasn't yet started, they now do a weekly catch-up. Both live alone, and both have been working from home, so what new information there is to share is limited, yet their calls tend to last an hour or two.

"I hate working from home," Holly says. "I might not mind if I had a better home setup, but they gave me a tablet. A fucking tablet. Not even a laptop. So rather than my big office with my big desk and my big computer, I have a fucking tablet."

"That's messed up," Ivy says. "We weren't provided with equipment, so I'm lucky I bought myself a laptop during the Black Friday sales last year or I'd be working from my ten-year-old iPad and I would want to gouge my eyes out."

They discuss how each of them is dealing with previously simple tasks like grocery shopping, what shows they're watching, what books they're reading, and on and on. In a brief pause in the conversation, Ivy decides to casually introduce a new topic.

"My neighbor has been joining Toby and I for our mid-morning walks for the last few weeks," Ivy says, having totally nailed the casual, breezy tone she wanted.

"Is it the chatty lady from downstairs? Is that safe?" Holly asks. "Because there's no way she's practicing proper social distancing."

"No, not Annie, it's a guy from upstairs. And we stay far apart and wear masks, so I think it's safe. His name is Jason."

Holly isn't fooled for a second. "Jason, huh?" Holly says, as if she is about to start singing, "Jason and Ivy sitting in a tree, K I S S I N G!"

"Yah," Ivy continues, casual tone still firmly in place. "He's nice. He has an older dog, so Toby has a friend to walk with, which is nice."

"That is nice. For *Toby*," Holly says teasingly. "I think it's great that *Toby* has a friend. It's too bad that *Toby* has been telling me how he gave up on 'friends' and was going to take this time during quarantine to really evaluate what he wants in a relationship."

"Ha ha," Ivy says, dryly.

"No, don't you remember? *Toby* vowed that he was done trying to please men and make broken relationships work and he was happy being single."

"Toby did say that. And he meant it," Ivy retorts with only a hint of irritation. "He just has a new friend. Just a friend. A male friend who is a self-proclaimed germophobe so even if he were interested in Toby, this would be a terrible time for a relationship."

"Eh. There's not a man alive who is going to prioritize germs over sex. But sure. Tell yourself whatever you need to so you can enjoy your time with your new, single, male friend who likes dogs," Holly says.

"I don't even know if he's into fat girls. And even if he is, I've been in full comfy quarantine fashion mode. Very unsexy. He's seen me wear Crocs! And I almost always have my hair in a messy bun. Not a fashion messy bun, an actual messy bun," Ivy protests.

"Well, it doesn't matter, you're not looking for another relationship, right?" Holly says in a lighter tone.

"No, I'm not." Ivy says flatly.

But Holly's sisterly teasing continues, "What's Jason's last name? You've got to start practicing your new married signature."

Ivy begrudgingly plays along adding, "I don't know. With my luck, he does love fat girls, we fall madly in love, and his last name is Hairydickhead."

"And then you'll find that his family is super traditional and doesn't believe in a woman keeping her maiden name. But luckily, Ivy Hairydickhead has a real ring to it."

"Maybe his family will allow a hyphenate. Ivy Collins-Hairydickhead."

"Oh yah, that's much better. That fixed it," Holly says with a chuckle.

The two finally hang up about an hour later, having continued to chat while Ivy walked Toby and got ready for bed. Ivy wishes Holly a good night and Holly replies, "Good night! Sweet dreams . . . of Jason!"

"Shut up!"

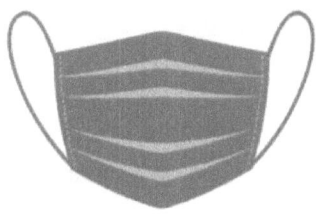

CHAPTER 11

The next day when Ivy and Toby go outside, Jason and Harry are already there. Ivy takes a quick look at Jason's thick dark hair and broad shoulders, as she does every time she sees him and is reminded of her conversation with her sister last night. She hopes the growing crush she is trying to suppress is not as obvious to him as it was to Holly.

The four of them begin their journey and are almost immediately met with a mentally unstable man sitting across the street on the curb, an unfortunately common occurrence in Los Angeles. The man is yelling in bursts of angry rants and though they try to ignore him as they pass, Ivy can't help but hear, "fat ugly bitch!" hurled her way.

She tries to continue their conversation with Jason as though nothing happened, but their usual banter is definitely off, so she decides to shorten their walk. They cross the street at a light just a few blocks away and as they reach the other side, Ivy hits the crosswalk button to cross the perpendicular street, but then doesn't stop to wait for the signal to change. Instead, she continues to walk along their established path.

"Are we not crossing?" Jason asks.

"Nah, I just wanted to trigger the light for that guy," and she gestures to a man in a Toyota who had been waiting for the light to change even before they approached. "That's a really long light."

And as they pause a moment, they see the light change and the man gives a "thank you" wave, which Ivy returns. Jason smiles and as they head home, he is determined to draw Ivy, not allowing any more awkward silences to intrude, he blurts out any topic he can think of.

"I need to decorate my place. I never planned on being there for long, so I didn't bother to really settle in. But now I've been there close to two years and I'm stuck inside and the bare walls are really starting to feel like a jail."

"I was going to paint before I moved into my place," Ivy replies. "I even bought all the supplies, brushes, rollers, coveralls, drop clothes, all of that. But then I couldn't decide on a color. And then I remembered that I hate painting, so I just left it. But I have hung up pictures and I do have knick-knacks and other decorative stuff. It really does make it feel more like home when you personalize your space."

"I agree and sometimes I'll get motivated to do something but then I don't know what style I like," he says. "I'll look at a painting and I like it, but then I think, 'Do I want to look at this *every* single day? Is that what I want my whole apartment to be based on?' and then I just don't get anything."

"Well, not to be a female stereotype," Ivy says, "But I happen to love shopping for home décor, so if you need any help, let me know."

"Great, I'll give you my credit card and you can go to town."

"I know you're joking but that would be amazing. Rather than maxing out your credit card, I can just go down a Pinterest wormhole and have a whole inspiration board for you by tomorrow."

"What is the point of Pinterest exactly?" Jason asks, mainly because he suspects a thorough answer will keep her talking for a while.

Later that evening, Ivy begins to search for interior décor ideas on Pinterest based on what she assumes a straight male in his early to mid-forties might like. She sends a few options to Jason, who replies in a timely manner, offering his opinions and encouraging more choices. After a half dozen genuine looks, Ivy begins to send joke selections.

She sends Jason a bedroom set that appears to be from the 1980's and inspired by a space station. It's hideous with dull gray, bright red, and black accents. The dresser, bedframe, and nightstand are all aggressively identical.

> IVY
> <PIC>
> Done! Look no further

A moment later she receives his reply.

JASON
That made me go blind

> IVY
> Ooo sorry!
> But hey, I guess you don't need
> to decorate now!

JASON
Problem solved
Thank you

They exchange a few more playful texts and Ivy ends the communication to take Toby out on their pre-bed walk. After they get back and she's in bed for the night, she continues scrolling through her phone, looking for real options for Jason, sincerely wanting to find items that make his apartment a home.

Still not clear on his style though, she decides to just send things *she* likes. Based on his feedback, she and Jason have similar tastes.

A couple of weeks later, on one of their walks, Jason proudly states, "I bought a throw blanket."

"Oh wow, I'm impressed," Ivy says, "Which one did you go with?"

"I actually bought the Gryffindor Snuggie," he confesses.

"No way! I sent that one as a joke!"

"I know but the reviews said it was soft and cozy and it just felt right," Jason says in one breath.

Ivy smiles. "I would love to see your place when you're done decorating, I suspect it's going to end up being a scaled down version of Hogwarts."

"That would be my dream home," Jason says with faux enthusiasm. After a slight hesitation he adds, a little more seriously, "What does your place look like?"

"My place? It's a mish-mash of stuff I like. There's no real theme or style. But it's homey."

"Like Lorelei's place on Gilmore Girls?"

"Maybe, I've never seen Gilmore Girls."

Jason stops dead in his tracks and dramatically turns to face Ivy. "What?"

"I've never seen Gilmore Girls?" she replies, somewhat sheepishly.

"Okay, your hatred for British comedy was bad, but this is inexcusable. It's on Netflix, what are you doing with your life?"

"Wasting it, I guess, based on your tone," Ivy laughs.

"This is the craziest thing I've ever heard, you need to watch it. Immediately. There's no way you won't like it."

"Do you think maybe you just built that up a little too much?" Ivy asks.

"I do not. I am *that* sure that you will like the show. When this fucking quarantine has passed, we're watching that. We'll marathon all seven seasons, though you should expect season seven to really shit the bed. But then there's A Year in the Life. We've got weeks, if not months, of Gilmore Girls in store for us."

Ivy's face already hurts from smiling and she feels a little warm flutter in her chest as she replies, "I'm in. 2023 is the year we watch Gilmore Girls together!"

"Aww, don't say that! Lockdown won't be *that* long!"

CHAPTER 12

The Morning Walk Gang, (as Ivy has dubbed them, only to herself. But she did briefly consider having shirts made) walk down to the park. Harry is having a good day, so Jason lets him walk rather than carrying him. Harry's determined pace makes Toby abandon his sniffing to lead the pack, getting them to their destination in record time.

When they reach the park, Harry walks a few steps from the cement path and sits down in a patch of soft grass. He begins to pant, and Ivy is momentarily concerned for his health, but he looks so happy she can't help but smile at him.

Toby takes a moment to check in on Harry and the adorableness forces Ivy to pull out her phone to capture this moment. Getting down in the grass with them, she takes a few pictures before both dogs decide to lavish her with kisses. Toby puts his front paws on her lap and tries lick her face while Harry remains on the ground in front of her, wagging his tail, a display of energy she's never seen from Harry before.

"Toby, darling, you can't lick my mask. It's not sanitary," Ivy says trying to gently grab and hold him, but only succeeding in pulling him closer so he's able to lick her neck.

In his growing excitement, Toby gives her one more enthusiastic lick on her chin, catching her mask and displacing it a bit. Ivy takes her mask off momentarily, kisses Toby on the head, places him on the ground, then shakes out her mask before putting it back on.

"He usually knows better than to lick my face, he's just so excited right now," Ivy says as she stands. With her face out of reach, Toby aims his affection at Harry who has taken a seat again in the long grass. Toby begins playful puppy activities, trying to coax Harry to play, but his efforts fail and he soon gives in and joins Harry in the grass.

"Well, Toby's excitement is understandable, it's not every day he comes to the park. Oh wait, yes it is," Jason replies, sliding his phone into his back pocket.

"But not with his new bestie," Ivy says. She moves her attention from the adorable dogs to her phone, scrolling through the pictures she just took before she was accosted. She stops on a clear picture of Harry and Toby touching noses, both their tails slightly blurred from wagging.

"Aww look!" She says, holding up her phone so Jason can see. "This is a good one."

Jason leans in toward Ivy's outstretched phone. "Aww, that's really sweet," he replies. "Can you send that to me?"

"Sure! I can also send you about 500 pictures of Toby if you'd like. About half of them are of him sleeping."

"He is very cute, but I think the one picture will be enough. I wouldn't want to offend Harry by having more pictures of Toby than him."

"Do you not have many pictures of Harry?" Ivy asks.

"Of course I do," Jason replies, "But I'd guess fewer than 500. And most of the ones I have of him as a puppy are actual printed pictures. But I did take pictures of some of those pictures."

"Very high tech," Ivy teases.

Like a proud father, Jason takes out his phone and starts scrolling. He shows Ivy a picture of Harry as a puppy, unbelievably small and fluffy, sitting on a blue couch.

"Oh my god! Look at him!" Ivy coos.

Jason scrolls to another picture, this one of a woman holding Harry up for the camera, snuggling him against her cheek.

"He's so cute," Ivy says and she hesitates a second before continuing, "Is that your ex?"

"Yep, that's Nicole."

"Does she ever visit Harry?"

"Nope, I got full custody."

Regretting having said anything, Ivy changes the subject, "Should we make them walk?" she says, nodding at Harry and Toby.

"I think Harry is done for the day, but we can head back now," Jason says, picking Harry up and placing him in his carrier.

As Jason gets Harry situated, they hear a cheery, "Hello!" being shouted from halfway across the park. They both look up and see Otto and Hildy heading their way. Otto is no longer carrying his selfie stick, instead, Hildy is wearing a harness with a camera mounted on her back.

"Hi," Ivy says, waving.

"I'm trying a new camera," Otto says, a note of pride in his voice. "This one can do some really cool special effects."

Otto continues to highlight the many advantages of the new, more expensive camera as Hildy wanders around. The camera, which is larger than the last one, wobbles around on Hildy's back, likely capturing shaky footage of grass, Otto's legs, Toby's anus, just a wide variety of undesirable images.

And finally, Toby begins to pull at his leash to get them to start moving again, so Ivy politely excuses the gang. As the they leave, Otto says, "So you guys are walking together? I'm so glad, I knew you two would hit it off. I have a gift for matchmaking."

Ivy and Jason exchange a look and decide not to clarify their relationship, each only offering a sort of embarrassed laugh. Jason gives Otto a final, "See you later," as they walk out of the park and Otto begins to direct Hildy's movements toward a couple of children playing with a ball at the other end of the park.

* * *

The next day, Ivy sits at her desk, unmotivated to work. She tries to concentrate but it's starting to feel pointless, her mind can't focus on stupid boring work right now. As her restlessness continues, she decides to throw the strict walking schedule out the window and take Toby out now. Ivy grabs her phone and texts Jason to see if he and Harry are able to join her and Toby for their walk a little earlier than is customary.

> IVY
> Going to walk Toby soon, do you guys want to join us?

JASON
...
...
Not today, sorry

> IVY
> No problem. Hopefully you can join us tomorrow. <smiley face emoji>

Ivy has a moment of slight concern since Jason has been happy to join them every time she's invited him. She hopes Otto's comments about matchmaking didn't make things weird for Jason. Did *she* say something offensive on their last walk? I mean, probably. But Jason's usually not offended by her. She watches the dots come up on her screen as Jason starts to type and she eagerly waits for his reply.

JASON

...

...

I had to put Harry down last night. He had a
seizure
I had to take him to the emergency vet.

As Ivy reads each line of his text, her heart sinks further and she
frantically types back.

IVY
I'm SO sorry. That is terrible. Si there
anything I can do?
*is

JASON
No
I'm just going to sort of sit here and sob.

IVY
I totally understand. Please let me
know if you need anything

JASON

...

...

Thank you.

Ivy releases her phone which she realizes she was holding in a death
grip. It's hard for her not to think of how heartbroken she would be if

Toby had just passed. She considers what she would want if she were in Jason's situation. Then, she has an idea.

She runs to her closet and digs out a bag from Home Depot that contains all the painting supplies she never used. She determinedly takes out the white coveralls with hood, booties, and gloves and puts them on. Ivy glances at herself in the mirror just long enough to confirm what she feared, she looks ridiculous. Like the Michelin Man and a condom had a baby. Condoms shouldn't have babies, it's counterintuitive. Oh well. Heading toward her door she turns to Toby, who is looking at her with a mix of confusion and anticipation, assuming it's time for his walk now.

"Sorry Toby, you're not coming with me," Ivy says, putting on not one, not two, but three masks then grabbing her keys, and heading out the door. She goes upstairs and knocks on door 20. After a moment, Jason answers the door and is, rightfully, taken aback. Even with his mask on, Ivy can clearly see his surprise.

"Hi." Ivy says, "I have three masks on, gloves, and this suit is straight out of the sealed bag. I'm clean and I've come to give you a hug."

Jason gives a half-hearted smile and pauses for a second before he steps forward and wraps his arms tightly around her with the intensity of someone who really did need a good old-fashioned hug.

Joined together, the two awkwardly shuffle into his apartment and Ivy manages to close the door behind them. They stand in the entry, holding each other for a minute or two, beginning to sway slightly before Jason eases his grip, steps back a little, and looks into Ivy's face (well, what he can see of her face).

"Thank you. I really needed that," he says.

"Of course. Do you want to talk about it?"

"Not yet. Let's hug just a little longer," Jason replies.

"Bring it in," Ivy says as she opens her arms again to welcome him.

After a few more minutes, they release each other, and Jason invites her further inside the apartment. Ivy first removes her bootie covered shoes and steps out of the established quarantine zone by the door then they both move to the couch. Without prompting, the details begin to spill out of Jason.

He explains that he was drifting off to sleep on the couch last night when he heard Harry make a weird noise. He looked over at him and he appeared to be shaking. When Jason went over to check on him, he could tell something was wrong. He picked Harry up and took him directly to the emergency vet where a technician took him straight to the back to be examined. Jason had to wait in his car. Not long after, the doctor came out to speak to him, letting him know that Harry was having trouble breathing and asked if Jason wanted them to continue with life-saving measures. Knowing that the prognosis was dim, and knowing how delicate Harry had become, Jason chose to euthanize him.

For this, Jason was allowed to enter the building and was taken directly to a room where a technician brought Harry out so he could hold him as the doctor gave Harry the shots to end his suffering. Jason explains all of this between sobs, wiping his eyes in an attempt to prevent his tears from soaking his mask, and Ivy manages to choke out some words of comfort through her own tears, having started to cry about three words into Jason's story.

"I'm so sorry. I know how much Harry meant to you. It's really hard to lose a friend like that," Ivy says, as she gives Jason what she hopes is a supportive arm squeeze.

Jason nods his head and places his hand on Ivy's knee, then picking slightly at the thin white fabric of the coveralls he says with a slight laugh, "You look fucking ridiculous."

"What? You don't like this look? I think it's super flattering." Ivy replies with a gently teasing tone. "It's very Stay Puft Marshmallow Man." Ivy stands to strike a few poses so he can absorb the full impact of her ensemble.

The two take a moment to let soft laughs overcome their tears. As Jason watches her pretend to be an old-school Sears catalogue model, striking pose after pose with as she points to something in the distance or stops mid casual walk, he begins to genuinely laugh. Which, in turn, makes Ivy laugh and soon they are silently, hysterically, laughing.

The next day, Jason texts Ivy a little before their usual walk time.

JASON
If it's ok, I'd still like to join you and Toby for
your walk this morning.

IVY
Of course!!
Give us fifteen minutes (ish)
I'll text you when we're ready

JASON
Sounds good.

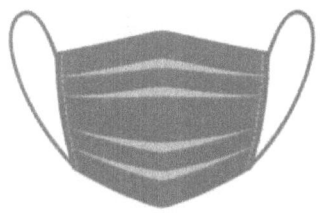

CHAPTER 13

Jason is already waiting when Toby and Ivy step outside. Ivy is immediately struck by the absence of Harry and fights against tears, not wanting to make Jason feel any worse than he already does. She manages to get out a greeting without having her voice break.

"How are you doing?" she asks.

"I'm," Jason starts, then sighs. "I'm not great. But I'm a little better. Thank you."

Ivy gives his arm a supportive squeeze in reply and then, changing the subject says, "Which way do you want to go today?"

"Let's let Toby decide."

They follow Toby as he chooses a route through the nearby historic fancy neighborhood. It's the type of neighborhood Ivy dreams of living in; house after house of well-maintained old homes with big old trees and immaculately manicured yards, many with classic white picket fences.

Jason is more talkative than usual, as if he needs to purge everything rattling around in his head.

"I moved into my apartment while I was waiting for my divorce to become final, which was a lengthy process. I didn't plan to stay here long," Jason says. "Before the divorce, Nicole and I lived in a nice condo in Pasadena. We were building a house in West Hollywood, an area she loves. I was happy in Pasadena and we were getting close to the completion of the construction when I found out that she was cheating on me."

"Oh shit," Ivy interjects.

"Yah. We were together for half our lives. I thought we were happy, but it turns out *she* wasn't. Anyway, soon it became clear that even counseling couldn't fix our problems. And then she left me." He hesitates only slightly at the end, but it's clear to Ivy that in the almost undetectable pause, he decided not to share something.

"Eventually, we decided she would keep the condo and I moved here to wait for the house to be done and everything to be finalized so I could move in, alone. To *our* house. In the city *she* chose."

"That's rough," Ivy asks.

"Yah. I mean, it was a great house. A friend of mine is in development and he has a really good crew. But as pretty as the house was, I realized I didn't want to live there. That was a place Nicole and I built together. We made it for *us*. Any time I went into the kitchen, I would have remembered that she chose those appliances to go with that countertop. She wanted the giant clawfoot tub in our bathroom, which I didn't care about, but she had some idea of having lavish baths in there, even though in the twenty plus years I've known her, I don't remember ever having taken a bubble bath." Jason explains. "Anyway, so I sold the house, and here I am. In purgatory, unsure of what to do next."

"I'm sorry. That really sucks," Ivy says. It might not be the most eloquent comment, but it really is the best way to sum things up. "Are you still thinking of buying a house?" she asks, realizing that she would miss him if he moved, but not letting her tone reveal that.

"At some point," Jason replies. "Periodically I'll look to see what's available and then I think about the reality of moving and actually living in a new home and I start thinking of all the things I don't like about the place, and I stop looking. I haven't even gotten a realtor. I didn't used to have so much trouble making decisions like this, but now I just feel like every choice I make is so monumental."

"I love looking at houses. When I was a kid, my mom used to drag me to open houses all the time and I'd imagine living there and already be picking out which bedroom would be mine and how I wanted to decorate it and then we'd go home and my dad would have to break it to me that we weren't actually moving."

"How many times did this happen?" Jason asks, with a mixture of amusement and concern.

"Oh dozens. I fell for it every damn time. I'm a slow learner."

"Well, it's too bad open houses aren't allowed right now, you could go look at places with me," Jason says, casually.

Ivy appreciates the hypothetical invitation. "Oh, I would definitely do that. Are there any must-haves that you know you want in your new place?"

"I don't even know anymore. I guess at least two bedrooms so I can have an office or guest room," he says and Ivy notes that it seems he isn't planning on starting a family anytime soon, which is nice to know since she has never wanted children. Just another thing they have in common. "My own bathroom," Jason continues, "I've really enjoyed having my own bathroom."

"It is one of the bonuses of being single," she agrees.

"What would your dream house include?" he asks.

"Oh my god, I'm so glad you asked!" Ivy replies, enthusiastically. "I've actually been thinking about this a lot lately. One might even say obsessively."

"Oh Okay, hit me," Jason says with a chuckle.

"Feel free to stop me when you've heard enough. These plans are extensive and pretty unrealistic overall. But, that's what a dream home is all about."

Ivy goes on to explain the residential compound she has imagined while in lockdown. There would be the main house, several guest houses for friends and family to live in free-of-charge, a gym, a fleet of practical but elegant electric cars for everyone on the property with solar and wind powered charging stations, and a Martha Stewart level craft studio.

And, of course, she has very specific features planned for Toby including a doggy door in her house that leads to a completely contained dog run so Toby could go out any time he wanted while remaining safe from coyotes, birds of prey, and dog-nappers.

"Oh and I want a hidden door to my office! Or to my bedroom, or the basement. Maybe all three!" Ivy concludes.

"Ooh, like a secret passage?" Jason asks.

"Kind of. For some reason, in my head, a secret room seems like a safe haven while a secret passageway seems like a way a killer can come in and murder me."

"Wow, you really have thought about this."

"Hey, some women plan their dream weddings; I plan my dream home. You know, so I'm ready when I win that lottery."

"Of course," Jason says, and on a hunch, he continues, "And do you play the lottery?"

"I do not," Ivy replies. "But reality isn't really part of this particular house planning anyway. This is absurd, the sky's the limit, crazy rich people house planning. That's what we're talking about now."

Ivy worries she may have revealed a little too much of her particular brand of kookiness all at once, but then decides to just let it all out, so she presses on. "I want the entire second floor to be my master suite and I think it would be fun if the staircase leading to the second floor was disguised as a bookshelf!" She glances at Jason to see if she can clock an expression. Masked, it's a little hard to read but she detects a little something.

"What?"

"Nothing," Jason says.

"No, there's something there. Say it." Ivy urges.

"It's nothing! The bookcase hiding stairs made me think of Anne Frank."

Ivy stops and faces him, putting her hand on his arm and looking him in the eye. "That was my *one* hesitation about that plan! I'm so glad you said that, I wasn't sure if anyone else would think that or if it was just me! I don't want people thinking of the Holocaust from something in my home!"

"In your imaginary home," Jason clarifies with a chuckle.

"Yes! I don't want to offend any possible future guests to my totally imaginary home! Plus, I don't want to be thinking about people having to hide in an attic every time I go up to my room."

"But I mean, if it's your house, you'd probably stop thinking about it," Jason offers.

"Eventually, sure. But if you and I both thought it, it's a bad idea. I'll figure out a good place for my secret door in my imaginary house though, don't you worry," Ivy says. "I mean, I do also think about what I would like in a normal home. My new life plan includes buying a home. No more renting. Even if I move in just in time to die from old age, I will own a home!"

"And put a secret room in it," Jason adds.

"Well, what I will realistically be able to afford will probably not be big enough for a secret room. But maybe!"

And a short but comfortable silence falls between them for the next several blocks as Toby leads them up and down street after street of beautiful homes and they both retreat into their thoughts.

After a bit, Ivy breaks the silence with a question that popped into her brain then jumped out of her mouth before she could stop it. "Do you ever want to be in a long-term relationship again?"

If Jason is offended by the question, he doesn't give any indication of it. "I really don't know. I can't even think about that right now. Honestly, I feel like I'm broken. I know that sounds dramatic, but I was with Nicole for so long and I don't even totally know who I am without her." Then after a pause he asks, "How about you?"

"One day, sure. But not now. It's obviously not a great time for dating," Ivy replies, gesturing to the mask on her face, "so I've decided to take this time to really reflect on what I want in my next relationship. And face the possibility that I won't ever find "the one" and that's okay too. It's actually preferable than being with the wrong person. So yah, I'm open to the right relationship with the right person."

Another contemplative silence falls, but a moment later Jason asks, "Do you want to have dinner together sometime?"

"Sure!" Ivy says, without an ounce of cool, but with genuine enthusiasm. "Did you want to do a picnic in the park or something?"

"We can. But I was also thinking, if you're comfortable with it, I don't really come into contact with anyone except you, and, not to be presumptuous, you don't seem to see anyone except me, so it seems pretty safe for us to be indoors together. Sans puffy white body suits."

Ivy feels an excited flush warm her face. "Okay, an indoor dinner sounds lovely. It'll be like the olden days!"

"*Olden*? You mean like before March of this year?" Jason replies.

"Yes, the 'before' times," Ivy says with a smile. "Obviously, my schedule is wide open, so whenever you want."

"Maybe Friday night? No, wait, you have your calls with your sister. Want to do Saturday night? I can make my famous lasagna."

Ivy ignores the twinge she feels that Jason remembered her Friday calls. She's maybe overly impressed with a man who actually listens to her and retains information. "Ooh, *famous*, huh?"

"Legendary, actually," Jason says.

"I can't say no to that."

They decide Jason will join Ivy and Toby at their apartment since it's better equipped for hosting. They can enjoy dinner and then watch Gilmore Girls, which Jason again assures her she will thoroughly enjoy.

Jason manages to snag a grocery delivery time slot after diligently checking online every half hour. He's excited to order every food he's craved over the last few months only to discover most aren't in stock. Luckily, all the dinner ingredients are.

CHAPTER 14

A gentle knock on the door and a whole lot of barking from Toby alerts Ivy to Jason's arrival. She puts her mask on, not ready to bare-face greet him quite yet, scoops up Toby, and opens the door. Jason is carrying a full bag of groceries in one arm and holding a couple of bottled beverages under his other arm. He is also wearing his mask.

"Come on in," Ivy says as she moves out of his way. "Let me take those. There's sanitizer right there," she says nodding her head toward the small table by the door.

"Thank you," Jason replies and he waits for her to close the door behind him and put Toby down so she can take everything from him.

Jason removes his shoes and sanitizes his hands, then meets Ivy in her kitchen. They have a slight moment of awkwardness before Ivy says, "I wasn't sure what you wanted to do about masks. We'll have to take them off to eat, obviously, so I don't know if there's really a need to wear them otherwise. But I'll do whatever you're comfortable with."

Jason hopes that this is the first of many occasions spending time in her apartment, so he thinks the masks might as well come off now, but what he casually says is, "I guess it's Okay to just not wear them."

They both take their masks off, with a certain amount of virginal shyness. It's the first time they've gotten a real close-up look at each other.

From her glimpse of Jason with Annie, Ivy had an impression that he was attractive. But until now, she hadn't realized just *how* handsome he is. Not conventionally so, his nose is a little larger and a little straighter than expected, but his features add up to one very pleasing face.

Ivy does her best not to stare at his strong jawline or perfect lips. But it's not easy. She makes a point of looking away to avoid being a real creeper.

Jason couldn't help but notice Ivy's beautiful green eyes the moment he met her. But he takes this opportunity to fully appreciate her up close and personal. He'd heard the term "button nose" before, but until he saw Ivy's, he didn't really know what that meant. Along with her full cheeks there's no denying Ivy is cute as hell.

Ivy watches Jason unload the groceries he brought and then shows him where everything is, pulling out the necessary baking dish, bowls, and utensils. She asks if he needs help with anything and, to her relief, he declines any assistance. He does, however, invite her to enjoy the sparkling water he brought for her, knowing she does not drink, and she gladly takes a seat at the kitchen table to watch him cook.

"So, is this a family recipe?" Ivy asks.

"It is. This is grandma DeSario's recipe, from the old country."

"Is that your last name?"

"It's funny, we've been talking for weeks, I'm in your kitchen cooking us dinner and we didn't really even know what the other person looked like, let alone our last names." Jason looks up from the sauce he is stirring and smiles at her. "No, that's my maternal grandmother's name. My last name is Johnson."

"Nice to meet you, Jason Johnson, I'm Ivy Collins."

Jason takes a small step away from the stove to offer Ivy a quick bow. "The pleasure is all mine, Ivy Collins."

They talk and joke and laugh and as soon as Jason puts the lasagna in the oven, they take their small salads and head into the living room, sitting on the floor to utilize Ivy's long coffee table as their dinner table so they can begin their Gilmore Girls marathon while enjoying their food. Ivy grabs the remote and as she gets ready to hit play, Jason looks around and takes in her living room.

The apartment is decorated with a variety of styles and colors, but everything is well-placed and combined in a way that shows care was taken. The pink velvet couch has a blanket and few throw pillows including one of a woven topless mermaid. There are enough knickknacks and decorative items to give the place personality but not so many that it feels cluttered.

"Your place is cute," Jason declares, "very inviting." Jason gives the couch another look. "Um, I'm sorry, what is this?" And he lifts up a blanket to reveal that it is, in fact, a Ravenclaw Snuggie. He shoots her a look of accusation.

"Well, it was a joke suggestion for *you*, but there was a reason I knew about it," she says, guiltily.

"So soft and cozy," Jason says, smiling at her.

Ivy gestures to the TV, "Ready?" Jason nods and Ivy starts the show. An idyllic town comes on screen with The La's singing "There She Goes" and Jason looks at Ivy and smiles. She smiles back and laughs a few minutes later when he enthusiastically sings along to the theme song.

The episode ends and it's time to check on the lasagna. Jason decides it's ready but suggests letting it rest for about fifteen minutes, but it smells so good they dig in after ten. They take a break in the show, choosing to eat this main course at the kitchen table, sitting in chairs, like normal adults.

Inside Ivy's warm kitchen, eating what is indeed a legendary lasagna, it's easy for them to forget about the trouble of the outside world. In here, there is no pandemic, there is no political or social strife. They are in their own little bubble.

***

That night in bed, Ivy feels Jason's hand on her hip. She grabs it and holds it to her chest, draping his arm around her. He responds by holding her more tightly, scooting into her so their entire bodies are touching.

"Are you awake?" he asks softly.

"I am now," she replies pushing back on him.

Jason moves her hair out of the way and begins to kiss the back of her neck. Ivy makes a soft noise of pleasure and releases his hand so she can flip over to face him.

She takes a moment to look into his warm brown eyes. They just watch each other for a moment, illuminated by streetlights coming through her bedroom window. Jason places a soft kiss on her lips, so tender. Ivy returns the kiss and is happy to feel his large hand cup her cheek. He moves his hand to her breast and begins to rub his thumb over her nipple. Prompted by her sound of pleasure, Jason rolls her on her back. Sitting up and straddling her, he removes his shirt and tosses it to the ground. He then pulls hers over her head, exposing her aroused, full breasts. He takes a moment to drink them in before kissing her again, this time with much more force.

Ivy slides her hands down his chest until she feels him, practically breaking through his pajama pants. As she strokes him, Jason moans into her mouth. Ivy is absolutely aching to have him inside her and as they start to remove their pants, her phone blasts a mood-breaking chime.

The sound, so close to her ear, startles Ivy out of her dream. She's slightly disoriented, taking her a second to realize she fell asleep on the couch. She'd reheated the lasagna left-overs, then sat down to rewatch her favorite season of Great British Baking Show as she ate.

She remembers having put the dish in the sink and then thinking she'd just take a quick little power nap, but thirty minutes later, she's sleeping so deeply that she can still feel Jason's lips on hers. Jesus Christ, daytime sex dreams after watching a baking show? Maybe this isolation is starting to get to her.

She looks at her phone and sees that Jason is texting about their walk time. She sends back a quick text saying she'll be ready in twenty minutes. Then she excuses herself from Toby and heads to her bedroom to finish off what her dream started.

***

As they begin their walk, Ivy turns to Jason and declares, "I think I'm pregnant."

Jason looks at her in surprise and manages to stammer, "I have questions."

"I'm pregnant with a lasagna baby," and Ivy holds her belly in the way pregnant women do.

"Holy shit, don't scare me like that," Jason says.

She has a second of curiosity as she considers what his response means, but she assumes it's his concern over an implied lack of isolation. Rather than following up with that, she says, "You can't just leave delicious leftovers at my place. I have no self-control. I will eat them."

"Good, please enjoy. I'm glad you liked it."

"Well, I shouldn't eat *all* of it, why don't you come over for leftovers. Or at least take some back to your place."

"I'll come over. We can continue our Gilmore marathon," Jason says.

"Perfect."

They decide that Jason will join Ivy and Toby tomorrow on their afternoon walk rather than the usual mid-morning walk, then continue their marathon, then have lasagna. As an extra special treat, Ivy will pick up some desserts from Porto's Bakery. She doesn't normally make plans on work nights, but right now, that rule can straight up go fuck itself.

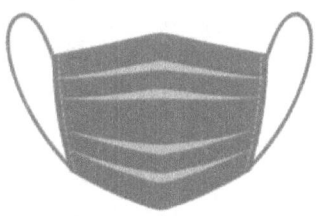

CHAPTER 15

Jason and Ivy sit down at the coffee table to continue their marathon and enjoy the reheated lasagna along with a fresh loaf of garlic bread, a surprise Jason brought with him. Toby sleeps peacefully behind them on the couch as Ivy steels herself to make a potentially awkward confession.

"Hey so, I didn't mention this last time because I didn't want to scare you off, but I'm guessing it's going to come up with this show at some point, so I want to warn you. I'm at that time in every woman's life where her hormones just become real dickheads. Because of that, I'm likely to start crying if anything even remotely sentimental happens in this show," Ivy explains. "So, feel free to just ignore that when it happens. I don't want it to be happening, you don't want it to be happening, but apparently, God does. So, you've been warned."

"Aren't you really young for menopause?" Jason asks.

"God bless you and your sweet mouth for saying such things," Ivy replies. "Yes, I am obviously very young and vibrant, thank you. But, according to Doctor Internet, the perimenopausal fun can start around forty and last for like a decade until the real shit kicks in. Isn't that cool?"

"An entire decade?" Jason asks incredulously.

Ivy nods grimly. "For some people! Hopefully not for me, but it's not looking great. I think my ovaries figured out a while back that I wasn't going to put them to their full use, so they've developed senioritis."

"That sounds very scientific, yes," Jason says, still processing this information. "I've gotta say, I'm starting to think maybe being a woman isn't all it's cracked up to be."

"Yah," Ivy replies. "It's not great. If it weren't for multiple orgasms, it wouldn't be worth it at all."

Jason laughs, "I'm glad it all evens out in the end. And thank you for the warning, now when I see you crying, I'll just tell myself, 'It's alright, at least she can come a lot'."

With Ivy's warnings out of the way, they continue the show and watch Rory suffer through a birthday party Emily has organized for her. This prompts a discussion between Jason and Ivy about their high school years, where they went to school, extracurricular activities and first loves, completely talking over the show, eventually causing Ivy to just pause it.

Ivy learns that Jason met his wife, Nicole, in high school band. Endearingly nerdy. He played drums, she played saxophone. They also went to senior prom together. They continued to college together and got married after graduation. Jason is surprisingly open about all this and the way he shares these memories shows genuine nostalgia. When he gets to more recent memories though, he shuts down.

Ivy in turn shares her complete lack of successful long-term relationships and her theories behind the long history of dating failures. "I haven't dated a ton, but I've been in enough relationships to notice a definite pattern emerging. For years, I assumed that when a relationship was struggling it was because I was doing something wrong. I needed to change to make things work. But I'm starting to realize that maybe the problem is who I'm choosing to be in a relationship with."

"You think you have bad taste in men?"

"Yes and no. I mean, more recently especially, I have gone out with some assholes, but even with some of the nice guys I've dated in the past, we just weren't on the same page with things, and I was afraid to really be myself around any of them," Ivy says. "Like I had to present the best possibly version of myself.

"Why have you been dating assholes recently?" Jason asks thoughtfully.

"Because women have a shelf-life and I'm past my expiration date so single men around my age, all of whom still consider themselves to be a real catch, go into a relationship with me with the idea that they're doing *me* a favor. Like I owe them something for the gift of dating them. My recent revelation is that I agreed with them. I felt like I wasn't good enough for them. So, obviously, that's something I need to work on."

"Yah, those guys sound like real dicks," Jason states plainly. "It definitely sounds like you haven't been following the Grail Knight's advice."

"I might not have chosen wisely each time," Ivy replies with an acknowledging smirk, "but I have never knowingly gone into a relationship consciously thinking, 'Well this guy is a real piece of shit, but he's better than nothing.' It just sort of comes out along the way. And online dating is a nightmare. They're all either obvious monsters or illusionists trying to create a decent human where there isn't one."

"I don't want to derail this conversation, but I do have to say, I'm so happy you caught the Indiana Jones reference of the knight," Jason says, warmly.

"Um, yah, of course. Last Crusade is the best Indiana Jones movie, and I watched it a lot as a kid," Ivy says, knowing she's going to get an argument about this claim based on the face Jason makes. But before he can comment she continues, "You don't even have to say it, I already know you're going to say Temple of Doom is your favorite. Being a straight male, and being your age, you're never going to concede that Last Crusade is best. But fucking Billie or Willie or whatever the hell Kate Capshaw's character was named was a truly, truly annoying character."

"I had such a crush on her," Jason says.

"Of course you did!" Ivy says, pointing at Jason in a gotcha gesture. "That woman is annoying, whiny, helpless, just terrible. But she's conventionally attractive so your adolescent male brain ignored all of that other shit and focused on her looks."

"I did think she was hot," he agrees.

"Sure, and that's fine. You were a kid and I'm sure her feminine features spoke to something inside you. Unfortunately, it seems that most men don't grow out of that base stage."

"That is a shame," Jason agrees.

"Also, a lot of men don't choose their partners just based on their own feelings," Ivy continues, "they date to impress other men. They're afraid their friends will make fun of them if they date an ugly woman. So even not particularly good-looking men want a beautiful woman and if they can't get that, they'll settle for a less attractive woman, but then she has to be a perfect, flawless girlfriend in every other way just so that when his friends see that he's with, for example, a fat girl, he can say, 'Yah, she might be fat, but she …' and then fill in the blank with why it's acceptable to date her."

Jason frowns. "This is something you've encountered with multiple men?"

"Yes! And to be clear, the list of other attributes doesn't tend to include things like, 'She's really thoughtful and intelligent!'. In a lot of my relationships, I felt like I couldn't slack in any area of my physical appearance if I wanted to be considered desirable. And that gets exhausting."

"Like a 50's housewife who tidies up the house in full hair and makeup in a house dress and heels," Jason says.

"Exactly! I mean, the 50's weren't *that* long ago, so we're still dealing with that shit."

"Well, I can see that we have wandered onto a topic you're passionate about," Jason says with a respectful nod.

"Yes!" Ivy says, still worked up.

"And I can't argue with a lot of what you've said."

"Yes. Because I'm right."

"But!" Jason continues, "I need you to acknowledge that-" and Ivy is afraid his next words are about to be a lame 'not all men' excuse and she's ready to roll her eyes in her most exaggerated manner when Jason actually says, "Men are the superior sex and we can do whatever we want."

Ivy is so surprised by the joke itself and his shit-eating grin that she lets out a loud bark of laughter. And maybe even a snort. But a totally charming snort.

Pleased that he made her laugh, Jason continues. "No, but genuinely, I'm sorry that's been your experience with men. And on behalf of all men, I want to apologize that we are often shallow dicks."

"Thank you. I know there are some guys out there, such as yourself, who are not dicks. But I sure as hell seem to have a dick magnet strapped to me, which isn't as cool as it sounds."

"Look, if you keep looking, you'll find the right guy. You're right, figuring out what you want is important," he says, giving her a quick smile, then looking away. "I don't want to shit on your theory, but in my experience, women can be shallow too. Some women will claim they appreciate how a man treats them but then dump their husband for some ripped piece of shit because he's got a take-charge attitude and a sculpted ass." Jason takes a drink of his water to punctuate his point.

"Yah," Ivy agrees, "Those women are real cunts."

This elicits an actual spit-take from Jason and Ivy can't help but giggle as she runs into the kitchen to grab him a couple of paper towels. "I'm sorry!" she says, "I shouldn't have said that while you were drinking. But the timing was just perfect."

"It was, I can't begrudge you that. But I'm sorry I just spit all over your coffee table. That can't be COVID-safe."

"Definitely not. I'm going to have to bleach that whole thing before I do my nightly table-licking ritual," Ivy says dryly. Jason begins to laugh. Then he laughs some more. Then some more until he's really wheezing more than laughing. Ivy is sucked in by his infectious delight and soon finds herself laughing right alongside him.

When their laughter subsides, both now pleasantly exhausted, they move to the couch, settling at each end, Toby in-between them. They restart the show, focusing on actually watching it this time, not just talking through it. The silence between them is comfortable and Jason sneaks a glance at Ivy to check that she's enjoying the show.

A couple of episodes in, Ivy is finding it difficult to stay awake. She isn't sure how long she's been asleep when she hears Jason's voice.

"Ivy. I'm going to go. I walked Toby for you. Good night," he says, speaking softly, as not to scare her. He then places a soft kiss on her forehead.

"Thank you," she replies, slightly groggy. "Sorry I fell asleep, it's past my bedtime."

"No problem. Go back to sleep," he says as he leaves, locking the door behind him.

She manages to offer a weak, "Good night," before the door closes.

When Jason returns to his place, he immediately feels lonely. His apartment, which was already feeling like a prison, is nearly unbearable with Harry gone. He feels at home with Ivy in her apartment and he instantly wishes he hadn't left.

What he wanted to do was just sleep next to her on the couch or wake her just long enough to move her to the bedroom where they could have just been in each other's company all night. He probably should not have kissed her on the forehead, maybe that was too intimate, but she looked so cute, and he couldn't help himself.

Spending time with Ivy has made Jason miss Nicole. His immediate thought after their first walk together was that he needed to tell Nicole about the new woman he met. A weird impulse, but it's just out of habit. Nicole was the only one he talked to about the real details of his life for so long. He wouldn't *actually* call his ex-wife to tell her about a new woman. That would be an odd topic to break their long silence.

His mom and sister would love to hear that he met someone, but he wouldn't want to get their hopes up about him dating again. Plus, his sister would tease him mercilessly. So, with all of these emerging feelings and nothing to do with them, he sits in his apartment, all alone, with nobody to talk to, thinking about a woman who he really likes but is also afraid to get too close to.

CHAPTER 16

"Hellooooo!" Ivy shouts into her phone in a sort of Mrs. Doubtfire way.

"Hello, friend. How are you?" Anthony replies.

"Oh fine. How are you?"

"Oh, just wonderful. I am on day 113, I think, of not leaving my house. So, you know. It's just fabulous."

"Booooo. I haven't seen you in person in forever!" Ivy whines.

"I know! I hate it! It's yucky! But with my shitty lungs, I can't risk getting exposed."

"You're being safe and smart. You're making good choices, little buddy! And hey, you've been stuck inside for over three months with your husband and neither one of you has killed the other. That's an achievement on its own. You're doing great."

"It definitely helps that Dustin still has to go into the office, so I get some alone time during the day." Anthony says. There is a brief silence, so he continues, "Just calling to check in?"

"Yah, nothing too exciting to report. I started watching Gilmore Girls."

"Oh, is that good?"

"Yah. I don't think it's for you, but it's cute," and Ivy decides to just go for it, "Jason suggested it. He made dinner and we watched it."

"Oooooo, that's so nice he made you dinner! What did you eat? But should you be having dinner in a confined indoor space?"

"He made amazing lasagna. And he works from home and only hangs out with me. It's minimal risk," Ivy replies.

"Is lasagna ever bad? I'm glad you have a friend you can see in person then. A little human contact is good," Anthony replies.

"I mean, bad lasagna would be a challenge, but I'm sure there's bad lasagna out there. Remember how we thought you couldn't mess up nachos until Casa Bonita proved us wrong? He is fun to spend time with," Ivy says.

"Still amazes me that a restaurant can fuck up nachos. Glad you're having fun, is it time for me to meet this guy? We could probably chance a socially distanced outdoor gathering. I'll make Dustin hose down our patio furniture. Hell, I'll even clean up all the dog poop."

"You are quite the host!" Ivy says with a laugh. "But I don't think either of us is in the market for a relationship right now. He's nice and a good listener though and he's funny and he thinks I'm funny."

"Well, he has good taste then."

Ivy ignores the compliment and continues, "If we weren't in the middle of a plague, he'd definitely be someone I'd bring over for game night for you to meet. But even without COVID, his timing is shit because, as you might remember, I'm taking a break from men for a while."

"Oh, how could I forget?" Anthony teases.

"I think he just sees me as a friend anyway. I don't know that there's any physical attraction on his end."

"But there is on your end?"

"I mean, he's a good-looking guy who can cook, bake, and has great hair."

"A winning combination! Has he made a point of clarifying that he's straight and/or single?" Anthony asks.

"Well, I wouldn't say he made a *point* of doing so."

Anthony sighs in mild annoyance, "Has he *mentioned* he's single without you asking?"

"Yes, he's divorced."

"He's interested in you. How long ago was the divorce?"

"Like over a year ago, I think." Ivy replies.

"Okay, so he's interested but probably cautious and likely damaged."

"That's just my type!" she exclaims sarcastically.

Anthony laughs. "Also, I would never doubt the sincerity of your declaration, but you've sworn off men before. I think a few men ago, if I remember correctly."

"Did I? I don't recall that," Ivy lies.

"Well, if you decide you're going to give men a chance again, this guy sounds like a good one. Let me know when I need to meet him."

"Well, again, I don't think he's interested in me in that way," Ivy says and Anthony sighs loudly as a reply. "But! If this turns into something serious, you will be the first to know."

Sure, Ivy has indeed sworn off men several times over the years. But what Anthony doesn't know, can't possibly know, is that she really meant it this time.

In her twenties, she just didn't know what she wanted, but it didn't seem like anyone else did either, so a long-term, serious relationship wasn't a priority. She was much better at filtering out assholes back then too. When she went out with her friends, the men who barely acknowledged her existence because they didn't want to fuck her were easy to weed out. Her thin friends didn't notice this classic dickhead behavior and often scoffed at her when told them the guy they thought they were falling in love with was a shallow jerk. And though Ivy never gave them their well-deserved "I told you so," all those friends found themselves heartbroken later when they figured out that they had made bad choices.

Then, when Ivy hit thirty, it was less of a group effort for dating and the dynamics changed. It was like men who were single in their thirties had just chosen not to settle down yet, probably for their careers, but women who were single in their thirties were damaged and running out of time.

That's when she started noticing the attitude shift in the men she would date, a shift in balance. Or, more accurately, a lack of balance. Ivy was in an age group that was, generally speaking, looking to settle down so it finally occurred to men that they might want to find someone who was more than just someone they wanted to fuck. But somewhere in the back of their heads, these men still whole-heartedly believed they deserved a beautiful, sexy, skilled, virgin slut, with that perfect balance of independence and total submission, so to accept less was to settle. Despite what they themselves had to offer.

Then one day, Ivy had an epiphany. She finally understood that her idea that she *needed* to find a man and settle down for her real life to begin was the problem because it made her willing to do anything to keep a man. Her whole life had been spent trying to please others and when trying to please men, she found herself constantly lacking.

This realization came just prior to lockdown, which was excellent timing. The quarantine has allowed Ivy an excuse to stay away from people and, along with that, to not worry about impressing others. She does her hair daily how *she* wants it to look, putting in effort to dry and curl it only if she's in the mood to do so. Same with her makeup. She wears big, thick, fluffy socks to bed with oversized flannel pants. She hasn't worn flannel pants since high school and rediscovered how wonderful they are, excitedly buying a half dozen pairs.

The freedom of not feeling the need to constantly be aware of her looks and to keep less attractive parts of herself hidden is something she does not want to give up.

So, she will continue to spend time with Jason because she really likes him, but it's best to think of him as a completely platonic friend. Someone she can be 100% herself around without fear of him not being attracted to something she does or wears because physical attraction isn't important between friends. Just friends. Okay, maybe they can be a little flirty and maybe even a little touchy, but she will not let herself fall for him. Besides, he hasn't given any indication that he wants more.

CHAPTER 17

About a week later, Ivy texts Jason to arrange for dinner and Gilmore Girls. They've already gone through the first season. She enjoys the show. It's charming. And if she had watched it when it first came out, she probably would have been a devoted fan. But now what she likes most is the quality time with Jason. During this lonely time, it's nice to have a safe friend to connect with in person.

They sit in their designated spots on Ivy's comfy pink couch and enjoy the show. A few episodes in a row deal with marriage and the topic is clearly on Jason's mind when he declares, "I really liked being married."

"Oh yah? You're not absolutely loving the dating rat race?"

Jason chuckles, "I haven't participated in that race since I was a teen and the years we dated before we were married were good. I would say I was happy for sixteen out of the seventeen years we were actually married. But then that last year was a real bummer."

"That's a pretty good percentage though," Ivy says.

"Yah, not bad. It's just hard because even when I think about some of the good times we had, I remember how it all ended so those happy memories are kind of tarnished."

"With some more time and healing, you'll be able to appreciate all those good memories again."

"I hope so," Jason replies with a forced smile.

"I'm open to marriage, but I realized that I've been living most of my life like one big to-do list. I've had in my head that, one day, I'll get married and then once I'm married, I can start really living my adult life and start checking off the rest of the list," Ivy confesses.

"What's on the list?" Jason asks.

"Travel, and not just back to Colorado or a weekend trip somewhere, but like big vacations."

"Anywhere in particular?"

"Iceland, Great Britain, basically all of Europe, I haven't gone anywhere!"

"I miss traveling. I haven't gone anywhere in years," Jason says longingly. "What else is on your list?"

"Own my own home. That's about it. The list isn't long or full of wild and crazy things. It's probably full of things most people my age have achieved. The thing is, I feel like I had a very basic childhood view of what my life was supposed to look like. Grow up, get married, honeymoon abroad, buy a home, have kids, retire, die."

"With hopefully a good amount of time between each of those," he says.

"Yah," Ivy says with a smile. "Not quite as rapid fire as that list. But then somewhere along the line, that timeline started to fall apart. Firstly, I realized I didn't actually want kids. Which felt weird to admit."

"I'm sure there was pressure for you to be a mom."

"Exactly, since all women are expected to want kids. And there's nothing wrong with wanting that, but I don't. Also, I do think kids are something you should really *want*. Not just an expected next step you don't even think about. I'm realizing I might never get married and I'm trying to figure out if I'm actually sad about *that* or if I'm just disappointed because I never imagined being able to have all the things I want without being married. Does that make any sense? I know I'm babbling."

Jason gives her a reassuring smile. "You're not babbling. It does make sense."

"But most importantly," Ivy continues, "I realized I should never have made *marriage* the goal, you know? I should have made having a healthy relationship a goal. Not just the act of marriage."

"That's an important distinction," he agrees.

"Anyway, my new goal is to live my life for *me* and if I happen to find the right person, with shared goals and interests, great! That's a wonderful bonus to my life. Not the key to it."

"That's some good self-reflection you've had," Jason says sincerely.

"Thank you," Ivy replies with a proud smile.

"Now that you mention it, I don't think Nicole and I ever even discussed whether we needed to be married, it was just what came next. Though I did like the clarity of marriage, a declared commitment. But you can have that without a license. And maybe it's better because then when it all falls apart, you don't have to deal with the shitty divorce paperwork."

Jason's slightly bitter tone doesn't change the mood, but it does return their attention to the show, both most likely lost in their own thoughts rather than fully paying attention to the show. Until, that is, Lorelai and Rory go on a road trip and Ivy interrupts the quiet.

"I never thought I'd say this, but I miss driving. I don't miss commuting or sitting in traffic just wanting to be home. But nice little drives while hootenannying? I miss that."

"I'm sorry, while whating?" Jason asks, chuckling.

"Hootenannying. Oh god, I hope that's not an offensive term, it's just what we called it in high school. Can't even remember who came up with it. But to hootenanny is to car sing."

"Oh, I like that."

"Specifically, somewhere between singing and yelling. With the windows down. And with a little choreography mixed in. We'd also often be in pajama pants and a hoodie, in the cooler seasons," Ivy explains.

"You must have been a real wild child in high school," Jason teases.

"Oh totally. There wasn't a lot to do where I grew up. No night life. So, we used to do really exciting things like go to the 24-hour Safeway and read the magazines or drive around on the backroads in the dark. Which as I say it, I realize was maybe not super safe."

"It's funny to think about the things we did as kids. I used to just take off in the morning on my bike and I'd return some time before dark. My parents had no idea where I was all day."

"Same. I used to walk to school in kindergarten unaccompanied by an adult. I don't know if that was because it was the 80's or because I lived in a small town or what. But either way, I was really cute, I definitely should have been kidnapped."

"Well, let's do it," Jason says. And in reply to Ivy's confused look, he clarifies, "Hootenanny, not kidnap cute children."

"Now?"

"Yah. Why not? Nobody will be out now and it's even cool enough to wear the uniform."

"Where should we go?" Ivy asks, loving this spontaneity. "We need to go somewhere we won't disturb anyone with our noise. We can't drive around here."

"PCH?" Jason suggests.

"Good idea. Is it okay if I drive? I get motion sickness pretty easily."

"Sure."

"That means you get the honor of being DJ. So, you actually have a very important job," Ivy says.

"That's a lot of pressure, but I'm up to the challenge. I'll go change and meet you back down here in ten minutes," Jason says as he heads to the door.

Ivy finds some clean flannel pants and her favorite soft hoodie. She puts both on and grabs two headbands and two hair ties. Since she still has time, she also brushes her teeth. Nobody likes a stinky hootenanny.

When Jason comes back down, he's wearing blue and green plaid pajama pants and a dark gray hoodie.

"Your uniform is perfect!" Ivy says, as she steps back so he can see that she is wearing a similar outfit with blue and red plaid flannel pants and a light gray hoodie.

"Are we bringing Toby?" Jason asks.

"Nah, loud singing plus the sound of the wind might be too much for him."

"I forget what it's like to have a dog with good hearing. Harry went deaf about five years ago."

They give Toby a "don't be sad that we're leaving" treat and quietly make their way down the hall and outside to Ivy's car. As they get settled, Ivy holds up the hair ties and headbands.

"Okay, hear me out," she continues in a public announcement tone, "With the windows down, and our mouths open singing, blowing hair can be a real safety hazard. That's why I suggest the use of one or both of these items to keep that beautiful mane of yours out of your eyes and mouth."

Ivy partially expects him to refuse these girly items, but he takes both and slips the headband on without hesitation. "I don't think my hair is long enough for the hair tie, but I'll hold on to it just in case." Ivy puts her own hair up high on her head to avoid issues with the seat back, slides the headband on for good measure, and they are ready to go.

As they take the freeways to the Pacific Coast Highway, Ivy explains that, traditionally, musicals or belting songs are really the best for car singing, but really anything they both know will work.

The first song they discover they both know is "Hold On" by Wilson Phillips, and as they drive past downtown it becomes clear to Ivy that Jason is a natural hootenannier.

An LA freeway's worth of songs later, they reach the coast and Jason selects "This Is How We Do It" by Montell Jordan. Ivy proudly shows off that she knows *all* the lyrics, not just the chorus like most posers. During a slight pause as Jason decides what to play next Ivy comments, "That song is the only song that can make me get up and dance at a wedding."

"Oh no. Are you one of those party-poopers who just sits at the table the whole reception?" Jason asks.

"I sure am."

"Half the fun of weddings is the dancing," Jason admonishes.

"Only someone who actually enjoys dancing would say such a thing," Ivy replies. "For those of us who do not like to dance, and who also don't drink, weddings are just a combination of the joy of celebrating your friend or family's love and devotion and being annoyed from having to repeatedly fend off peer pressure as you try to explain to people of varying levels of sobriety that you don't *want* to dance."

"But it's so fun!"

"Not for everyone!" Ivy counters. "People assume that those of us who don't want to dance are just shy. No, I'm not shy. If there's a song that actually moves me to dance, I will dance."

"And the only song that will move you is "This Is How We Do It"?

"Yes. And the few times I've given in and gone out on the dance floor when it wasn't that song, I have not enjoyed myself. I'm just out there thinking to myself, 'Right, move your hips a little more. Should your shoulders move more? Fuck, I think I'm off the beat now. When can I sit down?' and that's not fun."

Jason laughs, acknowledging that what Ivy has just described does indeed not sound fun. "To your point, I've never danced completely sober."

"There you go!"

"I feel honored that I got to see you do some dancing during this drive," Jason says.

"Well, that's also to your credit. You're choosing a lot of good songs! I'd be happy to have you as my hootenanny DJ anytime."

They continue a few miles down the coast, selecting a range of songs from various decades and genres and as the cold night air blows around them and the moonlight shines on the ocean, Ivy tries to remember the last time she felt so content.

"I think I need to take a song break," Jason says. "My throat is starting to object to this."

"Wuss," Ivy croaks, intentionally letting her voice crack as she looks over to give him a wink. He smiles back.

CHAPTER 18

"Oh fuck," Ivy curses as the reminder on her computer gives her a fifteen-minute warning for a meeting she had forgotten all about. Who the hell has a staff meeting first thing on a Monday morning? That is just messed up.

Thankfully, for these meetings, the participants are not on camera, so Ivy doesn't have to change her clothes or set up a nice backdrop or anything. She just has to sit through some mind-numbing boredom, with a few technical difficulties sprinkled in for flavor. A real recipe for fun. How many sound issues will there be this time? Which coworker won't realize they're not muted today? How many people will enter late and accidentally be on camera?

As she waits for the meeting to officially start, Ivy sends out a "Hello everyone!" in the chat to make it clear she's there. She decides her time would be better spent putting away her laundry rather than staying by her computer and watching her boss sit too close to his camera before he switches over to a never-ending series of charts and graphs.

She really does try her best to pay attention to what he's saying, usually. But if he can't make his presentation more interesting than laundry, that's on him, not her.

Ivy's mind wanders to how much fun she had with Jason this weekend. After they got back from their drive, they made tea with honey to soothe their throats and even though continued conversation certainly didn't help with healing, they talked about nothing until midnight when Ivy's yawning eventually signaled an end to the fun.

They both took Toby out for a quick pee so Ivy could sleep in a little and not feel badly for not getting up at 5:30AM to walk him. Before Jason went up to his apartment, there was a moment she really thought he was going to kiss her. But he didn't. Of course he didn't, he's just a friend.

Even after spending so much time talking, the next day on their walk, they had a long chat about their families. Jason told her that he regularly speaks to his mom and his sister, both of whom he plans to visit more when it's safe to travel again.

His sister and her family live outside of Boston and he FaceTimes with his nieces at least once a month, but every time he sees them, he's surprised by how much they've grown, and he often feels guilty that he isn't better about checking-in.

"My father was never really in my life," Jason explained. "My parents got divorced after my little sister was born, and I was so young that I really don't have many memories of him. As a kid, I resented him because all he left me with was a hard to pronounce last name."

"Johnson?"

"No," Jason laughs. "That's Bill's last name. I took his name when they got married, I was six. My dad's last name was Christoyannopoulos. Which, as an adult, I know is a perfectly fine name, but when you're a little kid, anything that sets you apart is bad. Even something as simple as a long last name."

"Kids can be little shits about that kind of stuff for sure."

"I don't remember anyone asking me if I wanted to change my name. My mom and Bill were getting married, and she wanted to take his name, and she wanted her kids to have her name, so she changed it."

"That's a lot of changes for a little kid. Did you always get along with Bill?"

"Oh yah. I don't think there's anyone on the planet who wouldn't get along with Bill. If I didn't have him, I might have really had issues about my dad leaving. But Bill has always been there for us and he's just a really nice guy. Very supportive. Much better at being a parent than my biological dad ever was."

"You still call him Bill, though? Not dad?" Ivy asks.

"Yah, for me, he's Bill. Because Bill is better than dad."

"That's really sweet. I'm glad you have him in your life."

Ivy, in turn, shared that she lost her parents in a car accident her freshman year of college, which is when she and her sister grew closer. Ivy moved to LA many years ago with a half-hearted notion of making it big in Hollywood only to discover she had no idea how to actually make that happen. Eventually, the need for steady income led her to a safe but boring government job.

As they arrived back to their building, they realized neither of them was ready to part ways, so they dropped Toby off and walked to Starbucks, their conversation still flowing easily through a variety of topics.

Ivy is brought back to the present when she hears her boss saying, "Are there any questions about that?" She walks over to her keyboard and types a quick "No questions" to prove she's still awake. As she goes back to her laundry basket, she remembers the Starbucks cake pop chilling in her fridge and takes a detour into the kitchen to grab that, but her mission is interrupted, not by the meeting she really should be listening to, but by a text from Jason.

JASON
I have been craving tacos all day. I think I'm
going to order some tonight. Want to join me?

> IVY
> Nah, I don't really like Mexican food
> JUST KIDDING!
> Of course, I want to join you

JASON
Here's the menu, I'm going to order around
5PM.

> IVY
> OOOO thank you! I'll place my order with
> you soon
> Should I get dessert?

JASON
Yes!

> IVY
> Any preference?

JASON
Nope. I leave it up to you.

> IVY
> <winking emoji>

A little before 6PM, Ivy stands at her kitchen sink doing dishes and listening to the Hamilton soundtrack. As "One Last Time" plays loudly in her ears, she starts to cry because of course she does. That song gets her every damn time. She puts her last clean dish in the drying rack as she receives a text from Jason letting her know the food has arrived and he will be at her place in a minute. Perfect timing.

As she lets Jason in, he looks at her and notices her red eyes. "Everything okay?" he asks with concern.

"Yes, just crying for no reason." Jason shoots her a suspicious eyebrow raise and Ivy explains. "I was listening to Hamilton and there's a song that makes me cry. Because that's my life now; I'm a person who cries alone over a song that has no emotional links or painful memories associated with it."

"Got it," Jason says. He moves into the kitchen and sets the food down on the counter. They decide to eat at the table since he ordered quite a spread and they need the room.

"Holy shit! Were you hungry when you ordered? This all looks amazing, but this could feed an army," Ivy says, looking at the many options before her.

"I've never ordered from here before so I figured I might as well sample everything."

"You're a smart man."

They dig in and the food is delicious. As they pile small amounts of a half dozen dishes onto their plates, the satisfaction of good food makes them both a little silly. Ivy does a happy dance in her chair with every bite of her carne asada taco and Jason laughs at her sheer delight, trying his own happy dance with each chip he dips in guacamole.

"I ordered a boatload of desserts and pastries from Porto's. But I don't think we're going to have room for any of them," Ivy says.

"There is always room for dessert. Maybe just much, much later tonight," he replies. And Ivy notes with satisfaction that he's clearly expecting to be here all night.

Ivy stops eating just a few bites before she crosses over into uncomfortably full, but Jason keeps going, determined to sample everything. Ivy leans back in her chair and wishes she could get out of these now very tight jeans and change into her lounging pants. And then she realizes she totally *can* go change her pants. She's home. Jason is a friend. Why would he care? Why should *she* care? Ivy excuses herself and returns in much more comfortable flannel pants with snowflakes on them, her biggest pajama pants, to accommodate her very full stomach. Jason looks at her change of clothes.

"I might have to go change into my pj-jammy-jams too. I can't stop eating these fucking chips," Jason says with deep, full belly, exhale.

"Now that I'm out of those jeans, I regret nothing!" Ivy says.

Jason finishes the last few bites left on his plate and, as Ivy cleans up, he goes upstairs to change his clothes. When he returns, Ivy has packed up all their leftovers and put them in the fridge and has moved their beverages into the living room, placing the Ravenclaw Snuggie at Jason's end of the couch and giving herself a blanket she finger-knitted a couple of days into lockdown. It's clearly a flawed first attempt, but it's still cozy as hell.

This evening, Toby has decided to stay in Ivy's bed, snuggled into the various pillows and blankets. Jason and Ivy begin to watch the show and each of them is uncharacteristically quiet and subdued.

"I don't remember going into food comas in my twenties, do you?" Jason says.

"I think this is a fun thing that comes with age," Ivy agrees.

"Seems silly to nap at 8PM, but I don't know if I can stay awake," Jason says with a yawn.

"I won't judge us if we happen to fall asleep for a little bit," Ivy says, her speech dripping with fatigue.

They decide to go back one episode, to one that they saw and mostly paid attention to and then set an alarm for forty minutes. No sooner does Ivy put her phone down, alarm set, than the two fall fast asleep. When the alarm wakes them, they find that Ivy has stretched out her legs, her socked feet in Jason's lap with his hands cradling them.

"Sorry," Ivy says, embarrassed and pulling her legs back.

"It's fine," Jason says, drawing back his hands, "didn't bother me."

They continue their Gilmore Girls marathon and since they napped, they're able to stay up later than usual, which conveniently allows enough time for them to be ready for dessert. A little after 1AM, they head back into the kitchen to choose from the ridiculous array of options.

"Do we have unhealthy eating habits?" Jason asks.

Ivy laughs and replies, "Yes. Yes, we do. But for now, we can pretend it's how we are coping with the stress of the pandemic and not a way of life. So that's something."

They select a few of the treats to share and sit back at the table. As Ivy takes a spoonful of a decadent chocolate mousse Jason says, "I was listening to a podcast today and they had this list of getting-to-know-you questions you can ask people you're trapped in lockdown with. Like beyond your standard conversation points, topics you might not generally discuss with someone. One of the questions was: do you believe in ghosts?"

"That's a good one. No, I don't."

"Me neither," Jason replies.

"Not the conversation starter they had hoped for, I'm guessing," Ivy says with a smile.

"I think you're supposed to expand on the answer a bit."

"Probably."

"I haven't seen a ghost and I think most of the ghost sightings and stories I've heard have another explanation like electrical issues, carbon monoxide, natural gas leaks, stuff like that-" Jason stops, his eyes going wide due to a faint strange noise he hears.

Ivy hears it too and smiles, knowing exactly what the noise was. "Or perhaps a beloved pet dreaming and making muffled barking noises in another room?"

Jason's face relaxes and he chuckles to himself. "Yes, exactly, like that; weird occurrences with reasonable explanations. So, it might be more accurate to say I strongly doubt the existence of ghosts," Jason says.

"Yah," Ivy agrees, "I'm not saying people I know who have said they have seen ghosts are lying. I think they do believe they did see a ghost, but..." and she fades off as if the end of that sentence can finish itself. "I also don't believe in an afterlife, especially in a religious sense. I think if there are ghosts, there is some sort of scientific explanation we just haven't figured out yet. Like another dimension or something like that."

"Do you believe in aliens?" Jason asks. "That was the next question on the podcast."

"No," Ivy replies. "I'm not saying there are no other life forms anywhere in the galaxy, but I am not in fear of aliens coming here."

"Oh see, I do believe in aliens," Jason says with complete conviction.

"Really?" Ivy replies with surprise.

"Definitely. I saw one of those alien history specials as a kid and I was convinced."

"One of those specials that claims since there are ancient drawings of people with elongated heads, it must be aliens?"

"Oh, I hear that tone of judgement, madam. And yes, it was."

Ivy laughs but listens attentively as Jason shares his extensive alien research and theories. When he has finally wrapped up his argument, Ivy has finished her share of the dessert and his has barely been touched, his determination to convince her of his beliefs causing him to abandon the sweets in front of him.

"I appreciate the case you've made," Ivy says after Jason wraps up. "And I'm glad we have finally come to a topic that *you* are passionate about. And I couldn't be happier that it's so incredibly nerdy."

"Hey, I've never claimed to be cool."

The next evening when Jason comes down to hang out, his usual rotation of a half dozen plain T-shirts paired with jeans is replaced by a black T-shirt that has "Nerd" printed in white across the chest and pajama pants with tiny green UFOs on them. Ivy laughs and compliments him on his bold fashion choice.

"Of course, you had that outfit just sitting in your closet. I love it!" she says with genuine delight. Not only does Ivy love how nerdy the outfit is, she feels validated since she's also gone for casual and comfortable, wearing a Care Bear shirt with her Valentine's pajama pants with the hearts and arrows. She makes a mental note to consider kicking up the comfort level the next time he comes over and putting on a sports bra instead of a real bra. Nothing says "just friends" like a giant uniboob.

They sit down on their designated couch ends with their designated blankets and Toby jumps between them, putting his face in Jason's to encourage pets before settling down next to him. Ivy feels something stir in her heart when she sees how comfortable Toby is with Jason. It takes all her willpower not to disturb them by grabbing her phone from the coffee table and sneaking a picture.

A few episodes into the show, Ivy pauses to ask a very important question, "Would you like dessert?"

"What did you have in mind?" Jason says, mock-flirty and waggling his eyebrows. Ivy laughs and waggles back as she lists the options.

"I could make pudding or cookies or-"

"Ooo what about that stuff from Porto's?" Jason asks.

Ivy blushes slightly. "Sorry, no. Those are gone."

"You ate *all* of them? Weren't there like four or five desserts left?" Jason says in what he meant to be a playful tone.

Ivy's demeanor instantly shifts, and her tone is icy when she replies. "Yes. There were. And I ate them because I wanted to. Do you have a problem with that?"

Jason realizes too late that he should not have said anything. "I don't have a problem with that at all."

"Great. Now, if you're done judging me, I'll continue with your dessert options," Ivy says in a tone that Jason is not familiar with, but which he might describe as deadly cold. Or maybe emotionless loathing? Or what he actually suspects it is, and what breaks his heart, hurt.

"I was not judging you. I was teasing you," Jason says calmly, making damn sure not to tip into patronizing.

"Fine. So, as I was saying, I can make pudding, cookies, or I have some frozen Greek yogurt bars. Which would you like?"

"Whatever is easiest for you," Jason says, meekly.

"Great, frozen yogurt bar it is." Ivy goes to the kitchen to grab Jason his dessert, grabs him a napkin, and practically shoves them into his hand when she returns to the living room, sitting back down on the couch.

"Are you not having one?" Jason asks.

"Oh, you're out of your goddamn mind if you think I'm ever eating dessert in front of you again, my friend." And she restarts the episode, looking pointedly at the TV.

Jason places his packaged dessert on the coffee table, gently moves Toby so he can get up, and stands in front of Ivy. She glances up at him but maintains her angry forward stare. Which Jason might otherwise find amusing since she's basically staring at his crotch, but in this instance, he knows better than to take this situation lightly.

Jason takes Ivy's hands, pulls her up so she is standing between him and the couch, and hugs her. As he holds her close to him, her arms still stubbornly at her side, he speaks gently to her.

"You can eat as many desserts as you want. I would never judge you. I really was teasing you, which was clearly a poor choice on my part. The reason *I* didn't take any of the desserts with me last night when you offered was because I knew I would eat all of them. And I was already planning on eating all the dinner leftovers, like a totally healthy adult who makes great decisions. I am really sorry I said anything to upset you."

Ivy moves her arms so she is hugging him back and she says into his ear, "So you're telling me you're one of those people who eats all the shit they want and doesn't gain weight? Are you trying to make me hate you?"

"If it makes you feel better, my cholesterol is quite bad."

"That does kind of make me feel better. I'm glad we'll both have heart attacks together."

"Should we continue the show now?" Jason asks.

"Sure," Ivy says, "Let's watch two more skinny bitches eat whatever the fuck they want with no consequences."

Jason lets Ivy go but looks her directly in the eye. "Can I please go get you a yogurt bar?"

Ivy smiles at him. "No, I really don't want any dessert right now. Thank you though."

They hug again to shake loose the last of the residual tension before both returning to their places on the couch, Jason having to gently move Toby out of his spot.

CHAPTER 19

Ivy walks into work a little after 6:30AM. It feels weird to be back in the office. Not just because it's been a while, but also because it's so quiet now with most of the office working from home.

She has some work to drop off and more to pick up, so even though she'd been putting it off, a quick trip into the office was necessary. Coming in this early certainly wasn't but trying to beat traffic is an old habit.

Ivy is in the office for no more than five minutes before Laverne comes over to greet her, in her Laverne way. "You're here."

"I am. But hopefully not for long. Why are you here?"

"Oh, I've been coming in every day. I'm not using my computer, my electricity, and my internet for work stuff! If the county wants me to work from home, they need to provide me with what I need to work from home!"

"Fair enough. Even with the non-existent traffic, I'd rather stay home with a slightly higher electric bill than come in when I don't have to. And those bastards know it," Ivy replies.

"Well, you have a dog. I bet he loves you being home all the time. I don't have any pets and I'm so close it's taking me about five minutes to get here now, and most people aren't here. I practically have the place to myself."

"I'm going to walk in here one day and find you running around like Kevin Bacon dancing through an empty warehouse in Footloose, aren't I?" Ivy says.

"No. I'm not going to be dancing," Laverne replies, in that tone where Ivy can't tell if Laverne knows she's joking or if Laverne herself joking. "I've worked here for 35 years and they've never done anything to make me want to dance."

"What? How can you say that? Remember those beautiful keychains they gave us a few years back with the department logo?" Ivy says, doing her best to put enough sarcasm in her words that not even Laverne couldn't miss it.

"The ones we got instead of a cost of living raise? I tossed that garbage out right after I opened it."

"I think mine might still be in my cubicle somewhere," Ivy says, looking around her three walls, but not seeing it. "Someone must have stolen it. Such a treasure."

"I doubt it," Laverne replies. Definitely not realizing Ivy is joking.

***

Ivy arrives back home a few hours later, staying just long enough to grab some work and send a couple of quick emails. She gets back in time to meet Jason for their walk. As she steps inside her apartment, she's greeted by a sleepy Toby who wags his tail and does a subdued version of his happy dance, obviously still waking up. Ivy drops her work at her desk and heads to her bedroom to change into her comfy clothes. Having worked full time in various offices and businesses for a couple of decades now, Ivy isn't sure how she managed it. Working from home is the only way to go.

Ivy and Toby wait for Jason outside, enjoying the cool but sunny weather. Ivy smiles when she sees Jason's UFO face mask. He was not kidding about his alien obsession, and it appears that he's now fully out of the nerd closet.

"I ran out of coffee; do you mind if we stop to get some?" Jason asks.

"I will never say no to coffee," Ivy replies, and they lead Toby on the route closest to the Starbucks. Jason orders lattes for both of them, on his phone, as they walk. When they arrive, he goes up to the makeshift drink station they've set up on the patio while Ivy stands back with Toby. When they both have their drinks in hand, they look around and with nobody nearby, lower their masks to take a satisfying sip of the fresh foam.

"Have you ever been to Jameson Brown, in Pasadena?" Ivy asks.

"No, is that a coffee shop?"

"It's my favorite coffee shop. I think they've reopened, but I haven't been there since lockdown started. But we should go there sometime, when we feel like driving that is," Ivy says.

"Another opportunity to hootenanny?" Jason asks, in a cheery tone.

"Yes! It *is* the best thing to do in a car!"

"That's debatable," he replies.

"The best safe thing to do in a moving car. While you're the one driving," Ivy clarifies, and Jason nods in thoughtful agreement.

They all walk at a decent pace, Toby showing no interest in sniffing and maintaining his happy trot, and when there is a pause in conversation, Ivy takes the opportunity to address something that's been on her mind.

"About the other night, when I got pissy," she says, "I want to say I'm sorry. That particular mood swing wasn't a hormone thing, that's just me. It's not my best trait, and I'd like to think I'm usually in a good mood, but quick mood swings are a possibility if something hits me wrong."

"Well, I'm still sorry I offended you. I didn't mean to do that. I would never intentionally hurt your feelings."

"I know and I appreciate your apology. I also appreciate you not running away when I was upset with you, I wouldn't have blamed you if you had excused yourself and never returned. I just want to be clear, it's not like the random crying, it's not just my dumb hormones. It's me. So, it's not something to dismiss when I have an actual reason to be upset. And it's not something to just forgive when I don't. I guess I just wanted you to know all that."

"Noted," Jason replies.

"And now, if there are any unattractive traits *you* have that you'd like to share, go ahead!" Ivy offers cheerfully, hoping to move on from any weirdness she might have created. But Jason doesn't seem weirded out.

"I guess you could say that I have the opposite problem, I just hold my anger inside. I'm bad with expressing my emotions, which I've been told repeatedly, by every woman in my life, is not healthy. But I could be pissed or upset and you'd probably never know it."

"Wait, are you mad at me now?" Ivy teases.

"Yes," Jason replies with a laugh. "I'm in a fiery rage right now."

"Oh man, you really do keep a cool exterior. But for reals, please let me know if I do or say something to offend you."

"I will do my best," Jason replies. Then changing the subject, he continues, "I have a call scheduled with my nieces tonight, but do you want to hang out tomorrow after work?"

"Of course. I think we only have one more episode of season three. Where does the time go?"

***

That evening, Jason sits down to his kitchen table, with his bare walls as his backdrop. He glances around his apartment for anything he can prop up behind him or anywhere he can sit that doesn't look so sad. But there really isn't anything. His apartment is legitimately bleak.

He starts his FaceTime with his sister. As soon as he connects, he sees his nieces sitting at their kitchen table, their smiling faces beaming. His sister stands behind them, trying to get them to sit down properly in their chairs. Their kitchen, unlike his, displays the clutter of a family. Jason smiles and waves at the camera.

"Hey girls!" he says warmly.

"Uncle Jason!" the two girls yell in unison, looking directly into the camera at the sound of his voice. As Jason leans in and looks more closely at the six-year-old, he sees she is missing both front teeth.

"Amy! Where did your teeth go?" he asks, with mock-concern.

Amy mugs at the camera, proudly showing off her imperfect smile and his sister, Angie, answers, "The Tooth Fairy took them."

"Oh yah? She took my teeth too, many, many, many years ago. You'd think she'd have enough teeth by now. Did she give you anything in return?"

"I got $5!" Amy says with delight.

"What? The Tooth Fairy only ever gave me a quarter. You must have much better teeth than I did," Jason says playfully. And as he notices his other niece beginning to zone out, he says, "How are you, Sammi?"

The four-year-old has been staring down at something she's holding in her lap but looks up at the sound of her name and he sees that her lips are juice stained. She smiles at him, shyly, and he gives her a big genuine smile back.

"Sammi has a new bracelet," Angie says. "We made jewelry today from macaroni and yarn. Show your uncle."

"Can I see it?" Jason asks and Sammi holds it up for the camera. "That is beautiful. Did you make mommy any jewelry? I don't see her wearing any," and he grins at Angie. She begrudgingly smiles back, knowing he's trying to cause trouble.

Angie shoots him a knowing glance and, stepping back a little further behind the girls, flashes her brother double middle fingers and mouths "fuck you" for emphasis before seamlessly popping back into the call. "Mommy was wearing it earlier, but had to take it off to make dinner," Angie replies.

"Why aren't you wearing it now, Mommy? You're done with dinner, right?" Jason says, smiling.

Angie gives him a death stare but all he can do is laugh mischievously before he leads the girls in a chant for her to "Put the necklace on! Put the necklace on!" Angie begrudgingly gets up, moves off camera for a moment, and returns wearing a long macaroni necklace that has been sloppily adorned with fake jewels and some glitter, most of which is already falling onto her shirt and the table.

"Oh Mommy, you look like a queen!" Jason says with exaggerated awe and the girls giggle with glee.

"Take note, if you're looking for gifts for me, I need a matching bracelet and ring," Angie says to Jason.

"I will make sure to text Santa immediately," Jason replies.

"Uncle Jason!" Amy shouts.

"Yes, my dear?"

"Where's Aunt Nicole?" Amy says, and Angie tenses up just long enough to shoot a glance at Jason to get his reaction before quickly changing the subject.

"Hey girls, why don't you go grab three toys you want to show Uncle Jason and bring them back here? Three toys, ready, set, go!" Angie says and the girls excitedly run out of the room. Angie continues to the camera.

"I'm sorry, Amy found that teddy bear Nicole gave her when you guys were here last and she was asking about her. I tried to explain, but you know."

"It's really okay," Jason replies.

"They're probably going to forget to come back here, so we have some time. How else have you been, staying busy with work?" Angie asks.

"Yah. I'm good and work is good."

"Mom is worried about you."

Jason doesn't answer but makes an exaggerated shocked face straight into the camera.

"Fair enough, but should *I* be worried about you?" Angie asks.

"No. I've actually been pretty good, all things considered. An occasional sob here and there, but definitely at decreasing frequency."

"There you go, celebrate the small victories," Angie says teasingly.

Jason loves his sister. These calls are always tricky for him because he wants to catch up with her and with his nieces but it's also difficult for him to hide things from Angie. Most people can't see any difference in his demeanor, but she can. It makes him feel he has to be extra careful around her. Which in turn, probably lets her know there's something he's trying to hide.

"Enough about me," Jason says, "How are you? How's Carol?" He says the name with special emphasis, knowing that the mere mention of Angie's HOA nemesis is the perfect way to change the subject.

Angie goes on for a bit about Carol's antics before the girls return, Amy with one toy to show Jason, Sammi empty-handed. He talks to them for a while and does his best to engage but after about ten more minutes, it's clear that the girls have reached the end of their attention spans.

With a lot of enthusiastic and ear-piercing good-byes, they end the call. And the quiet of Jason's apartment is deafening.

CHAPTER 20

The menu for the evening was discussed in advance. Ivy picked up groceries while Jason made his grandma's Italian dressing for two giant salads.

When on her own, Ivy has been surviving mostly on frozen meals and half-hearted sandwiches while Jason continues a menu of canned goods, mainly due to laziness but with a little bit of anti-social feelings sprinkled in for fun.

He recaps his call with his sister for Ivy, leaving out the awkwardness of the ex-aunt inquiries but making it clear to Ivy with every detail he shares that he loves his sister and his nieces very much.

After dinner, Ivy goes to her room to retrieve the blankets she washed but hadn't gotten around to taking out of the laundry basket. She hands Jason his Snuggie which he slips his arms into as he nestles into his spot, adjusting the pillows for maximum comfort. Ivy then places Toby's blanket, a small, knitted blanket Holly made just for him (which shows a great deal more skill than the blanket Ivy made herself) in the middle spot on the couch, just in case Toby decides to join them. And finally, her blanket, which she wraps herself in before plopping down.

Cozy and enjoying the scent of fresh laundry, they pick up where their marathon left off, Rory's graduation. The beginning of the episode is fun and quirky, but the ceremony itself is sentimental and sweet. Ivy feels her eyes begin to fill with tears, and mentally tries to talk herself out of it.

You've warned him about this, but there's going to be a limit to how many times you can cry in front of him for no reason before he thinks you're just insane. Get it together.

But her inner chiding does nothing to prevent the tears. Ivy subtly glances over at Jason to see if he's noticed her frequent eye-wiping and she sees that he is tearing up too. She pauses the show and reaches out to squeeze his knee. "Did I give you my peri?"

Jason smiles back but is clearly more upset than Ivy's own hormonal knee-jerk reaction, so her tone changes from teasing to caring. "Do you need a hug?"

Jason shakes his head.

"Do you want me to fast-forward? We can skip to the next episode if you want."

Jason shakes his head again.

"Do you want me to shut the fuck up and go back to watching the show?" Ivy asks with a teasing smile.

Jason laughs slightly and nods, offering her a smile as he wipes a tear from his cheek.

"On it!" Ivy hits play and directs her attention back to the TV, letting her tears stream down her face for a moment before getting up to get each of them a tissue, placing the box on the coffee table in front of them.

A little while later, they've gone a full episode without further tear-filled incidents. Before the next episode starts, Ivy says, "I should probably take Toby out now. Do you want to come with us?"

Jason can't answer this simple question. He's got a lot swirling around in his head. A lot of conflicting feelings. He wants to be alone and also doesn't want to leave Ivy.

He's feeling very vulnerable for some reason. What sounds perfect right now is to walk with Ivy and hold her hand and just continue to be next to her. Not talking, just being next to her. But he also knows that would be a little weird and that he's not going to be very good company right now. His delay in answering is obvious and Ivy interprets this as him feeling badly about wanting to say no.

Wanting to relieve Jason of any feelings of guilt or obligation, Ivy says, "You don't have to, we'll be fine. Get your butt to bed."

Jason decides to accept the excuse Ivy has supplied. "Thanks, I'm pretty tired."

He waits as Ivy gets Toby ready to go out, watching the traditional dance of Toby avoiding his harness. Then she and Jason mask up and walk out of her apartment together. They all stop when it's time for them to part ways at the stairs.

"Good night," Ivy says quietly so the neighbors don't hear. "Let me know when you're free for some more Gilmore fun."

Jason lowers his mask and gives her a quick smile and kisses her on the forehead, the only exposed part of her face before gently wishing her, "Good night."

✳✳✳

Back in his own apartment, Jason immediately knows he was right. This was not the correct choice. He is miserable in here. He takes off everything he needs to leave in his quarantine zone and heads over to his couch, sliding into his own Snuggie and settling in.

The rush of emotions he felt this evening caught him off guard. He was enjoying the show and enjoying being at Ivy's, just like always. Then, the graduation scene came up and he started thinking about graduating from college and Nicole and how it had sort of signaled the start of their adult life together. And without understanding what was happening, he became more aware of his feelings and less of his actual surroundings. Then, he felt his eyes fill with tears and there was a pressure in his chest he wasn't familiar with.

His immediate thought was that he needed to get it together before Ivy noticed, but then she *had* noticed, and it was fine. She hadn't freaked out. There was no evidence that she had judged him at all.

Still, he didn't want to extend their evening too much longer just in case his emotions got the better of him again. So here he was. Alone in his sad apartment.

CHAPTER 21

After hours of tossing and turning, Jason can't take it anymore. He gets out of bed and goes to the kitchen to get some water and maybe a CBD gummy to go with the melatonin he already took. Anything to just let him go the fuck to sleep.

He finishes the glass of water and just stares into the sink. He's painfully aware that he's doomed to stay awake all night. His brain is wide awake with no sign of calming down. Then he has a thought. Knowing he shouldn't, he grabs his keys, puts on his shoes, and heads down to Ivy's apartment.

She gave him a key to her apartment, just in case of emergencies. And just in case she got stuck at work and Toby needed to be fed or walked. Not so he could just let himself in. But if he knocked first, would it be that bad? Before he knocks, before he wakes her and Toby at this unacceptable hour, he texts her a warning.

JASON
Are you awake?
I'm about to knock on your door
It's not an emergency
I just couldn't sleep
And I don't want to be alone

He doesn't really expect her to be awake to see the text. But he wants to try to prevent any concern or panic she might have at hearing someone at her door in the middle of the night. He considers just going back upstairs because he's starting to realize what a stupid idea this was, but to his surprise, she does reply.

IVY

It's unlocked. Come on in.

Jason smiles because he realizes she expected him back. Otherwise, she would have locked the door. She always locks the door. Maybe she *wanted* him back. He enters the apartment, taking off his shoes and locking the door behind him. He hears Ivy's voice from her bedroom.

"Come here," she says in a softer tone than he's used to hearing from her. Or maybe she's still groggy from sleep. Either way, he's already hard.

When he walks into her bedroom, she isn't in her bed like he expected. She's standing at the end of the bed, her long blonde hair, usually up in a knot, is down, cascading over her shoulders, creating an ethereal halo around her inviting smile. She's wearing a long T-shirt that barely covers her. The thin fabric pulls tightly across her breasts.

"I'm glad you're back. Lie down," Ivy instructs.

Jason does as he's told and as soon as his head hits the pillow, Ivy moves slowly toward him, slowly crawling up his body, trapping him beneath her. When she's face to face with him, she stops, looming over him, observing her prey.

"Why'd you leave?"

"I don't know," Jason replies.

Ivy lowers her head and begins to kiss his lips with an eager force that he immediately returns. Jason reaches up to touch her body, anywhere he can. He's been resisting the urge to touch her for months and he can't believe he finally gets to run his hands over her soft skin.

He moves his kisses down her neck and to her chest, removing her shirt to expose her large breasts barely contained in a shiny, pale, pink bra. He reaches for them, pulling her bra down and beginning to suck one nipple, then the other. Ivy lets out a pleasurable squeal then sits back a moment to fully remove her bra.

He grabs her and pulls her back down on top of him, her body covering him. He kisses her passionately and before he knows it, she has moved back down his body, reaching into his pants to expose him.

She hungrily puts him in her mouth causing him to make a guttural, animal noise of pleasure. It's been so long for him, and he knows he's going to finish too soon if she continues like this, so when she glances up at him and they make eye contact, he smiles at her and puts his hand up to tell her to slow down.

Ivy stops, with a grin, sitting up, his body between her knees. In a swift and confident move, Jason sits up too, turns her around, bends her over and pulls her barely-there underwear down to her knees. He finds himself kneeling behind her, his hands squeezing each full cheek of her plump ass. She looks over her shoulder and teasingly says, "What are you going to do now?"

"You'll see," Jason replies and then he swings his right hand back to slap her hard on her right cheek. She makes a high-pitched noise of pleasure, so he does it again. "Do you like that?" Jason asks.

"Yes!" Ivy exclaims.

"I bet you do." He's waited long enough. He takes his rock-hard cock and taps it against her cheeks before he assertively enters her warmth. But the moan of pleasure he was expecting doesn't come.

"Wrong hole! Wrong hole!" Ivy squeaks with a start.

"Oh my god, I'm so sorry!" Jason says, as he quickly removes himself. "Are you okay?"

"Yes, I'm fine!"

"Are you sure?" he asks, still panicked.

"Yes. But if you have shit on your dick, that's your own fault!" Ivy says.

The two make eye contact and begin to laugh hysterically. Jason collapses on her naked body and they are laughing so hard, he feels her shoulders and chest move beneath him. His own body is shaking so much from the deep laughter that he wakes himself, a laugh still in his throat. It takes a second for him to orientate himself and realize he is alone in his bed. Though still quite hard.

He laughs again, knowing he has never and would never in his life slap a woman's ass and say, "Do you like that?" And if Ivy made that fake girlish voice in real life, he would lose his erection immediately. He makes a mental note to cut back on the porn for a while.

The next day, Jason is having trouble forgetting his dream. It was too vivid; he feels a little bit like a creep and decides to stay away from Ivy today. But by the time evening rolls around, he's feeling fitful like he just needs to be somewhere else with someone. At the same time, he's still feeling very anti-social. He decides to text Ivy with an idea.

JASON
I have a proposal

> IVY
> I do!!
> <diamond ring emoji>
> JK
> Please go on

JASON
I am in a weird mood. I don't feel chatty but I can't be alone in my apartment anymore
Can I come hang with you at your place, but we just play on our phones?

There's a long enough delay in her response to convince Jason he's made a big mistake and Ivy now thinks he's a creepy weirdo.

> IVY
> I've never wanted anything more
> Come on down!
> You're the next contestant on the Price
> Is Right

JASON
I'm bringing snacks

> IVY
> <emoji with hearts for eyes>
> I'll unlock my door and Toby is asleep in
> the other room, so just come on in
> whenever you get here

This text gives Jason a moment of pause as he recalls his dream, but he tries to clear that out of this mind and simply replies.

JASON
See you in a sex
*sec!
<face with hand over mouth and rosy
cheeks>

IVY
<face with wide open eyes and flushed cheeks>
Don't worry, it happens to everyone
Nothing to be ashamed of

Jason arrives about ten minutes later, one arm full of various treats, which he sets out on the coffee table. As Ivy stays on the couch, obviously comfy and feeling no need for a formal greeting, Jason gets them napkins and drinks from her kitchen and snuggles into his end of the sofa. He can't help but notice how cute Ivy's looking this evening, her warm smile instantly making him feel less lonely.

The TV is paused on a beautiful waterfall and as Ivy holds the remote, she explains, "So, this is my new Netflix go-to. This is Moving Art. It's just pretty. I turn the music down, nearly muted, and I almost completely ignore it while I listen to a book and play games on my phone. It's basically pointless to have it on, but it just feels right."

"Perfect," Jason replies, and seeing that she has one earbud in, he pulls out his own earbuds from his hoodie pouch. They stretch their legs toward each other on the couch, easily sharing the space and their blankets.

They pass several hours contentedly not talking. At his usual pre-bed walk time, Toby comes into the living room and stares at both of them. Ivy takes the hint and gets up to change into her standby "going out in public" jeans and T-shirt. Jason joins them even though he is clearly in his pajamas and doesn't feel like going back to his place to change.

Ivy considered staying in her pj's too, but she didn't want to give any of the neighbors the wrong idea. Especially if Otto was out with Hildy or Annie was wandering the halls.

As they wait for Toby to stop sniffing a particularly enticing spot in the grass, Ivy tells Jason about the mystery novel she's been listening to. He, in turn, shares that he is re-listening to an old favorite of his, a British comic fantasy, alternate history, mystery series. Ivy takes note and adds it to her phone's library.

When they get back to Ivy's apartment, they chat a little longer while enjoying a few snacks then they go back to their spots on the couch and their phones.

Around midnight, Ivy begins yawning enough for Jason to notice, even with his attention on his phone. Watching her try to stay awake, he speaks before he can even think about it. "I have another proposal."

"I do!" Ivy says, smiling. "It's funny every time. Go ahead." But Jason pauses, obviously wondering if he should actually continue. Ivy is intrigued. "Oh wow, this must be a good proposal. Tell me!"

"If you are comfortable with it. And it's totally fine if you're not. And please don't feel like you are in any way obligated-" Ivy cuts him off.

"Were you about to ask if I want to have a totally platonic sleep over?"

Jason smiles in reply, relieved that she suggested what he was hesitant to spit out. "Yes. Do you?"

"I do! But I should warn you. I snore. Not all the time, but when I do, apparently, it's quite bad. Like drunk bear with allergies bad."

Jason smiles again, "I can handle it."

"Then I'll get ready for bed, you go get ready for bed, meet me back here in twenty minutes. Go!"

Jason heads up to his place to brush his teeth and freshen up while Ivy begins her girly nightly skin routine. By the time Jason returns, Ivy has just begun to remove the massive number of pillows from her bed, placing them in her chair. The two get ready to settle in, Jason having brought down his own pillow.

"I know this is weird," Ivy says, "But I don't sleep under my covers. You're welcome to, the sheets are clean, but I sleep on top of them with this," and she holds up an ugly green over-sized throw blanket. "I know it's hideous, but it's soft and the perfect weight; I'm never too hot or too cold."

"Sure, magic blanket, I get it," Jason says with matter-of-fact acceptance.

They both get on the bed, Jason choosing to sleep on the covers as well, using the Snuggie from the living room, and Ivy asks, in a purely practical, logistical tone, "Platonic snuggle or stay separated?"

"Snuggle. At least at first, probably not all night," Jason replies.

"Big spoon or little spoon?"

"Little, please," Jason replies meekly.

They each shift onto their sides and Ivy scooches in behind him, wrapping her free arm around him, her hand on Jason's chest and her cheek tucked into his back. They each let out a deep breath and are asleep within minutes.

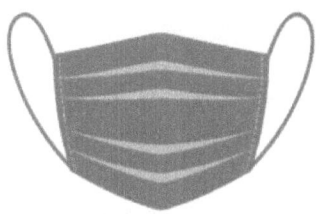

CHAPTER 22

The slumber party was a success. They both slept well, Jason promising Ivy he didn't notice her snoring, and it felt good to have the company. They walk to Starbucks nice and early with Toby, their hoodies somewhat hiding that they hadn't properly gotten ready for the day yet.

When they get back to her apartment, Ivy glances through her work email to see if there's anything she urgently needs to respond to when Jason reluctantly excuses himself to go get ready for some meetings.

A little later, Ivy gets a text from Jason letting her know he has "some family stuff" he needs to attend to and will be gone for a while.

When Jason arrives at his destination and has more time to explain where he's gone and why, he sends her another message. Turns out, he received a call from his mom around noon, interrupting his meeting. It was unusual for her to call at that time, so he immediately knew something was wrong.

She called to tell Jason that his stepfather had been taken to the hospital. Jason was packed and on the road within the hour.

Jason explains that they thought his stepdad might have had a heart attack, and of course everything about getting him to the hospital and seen was made more difficult by COVID. Ivy thanks Jason for the update and lets him know he can text or call anytime if he needs anything from her. She doesn't hear much from him after that for a few days. Which is understandable, he's with his family.

Ivy is pleasantly surprised by how quickly she goes back to her solo quaroutine. Back to her lone walks, back to making dinner alone. She congratulates herself because holding back and not letting herself think of Jason as anything more than a friend makes this abrupt separation less painful.

That being said, she does maybe indulge in cuddling his pillow a little that first night, breathing in his scent as she drifts off to sleep. In the morning, however, she decides to wash his pillowcase and the Snuggie so when Jason returns, he'll find laundered items waiting for him. But more importantly, she isn't tempted to do any more pining.

Jason is gone for two weeks, and Ivy endures the beginning of fire season in California on her own. This year, there are several fires nearby and the air is thick with the scent of smoke and char even through her thick face mask. The cars on the street are covered in a thin layer of ash and there are a few days when the sun is blocked out by the smoke, leaving everything in an odd orange haze.

Her close proximity to disaster actually somehow makes sense with how the year is going. A pandemic isn't enough. A chaotic government and fractured societal bond aren't enough. Why not add fire too?

Ivy orders extra filters for her air purifier, a bulk box of eye drops, and hunkers down for whatever the world brings next. Please don't let it be pestilence, she thinks. She really hates bugs.

After the first few days away, Jason begins to text more frequently. First, he lets her know his stepdad did not have a heart attack after all. Which is a relief. But he will still be in the hospital for some testing for another day or two and Jason does not want to leave his mom until his stepdad is back home and settled in.

Through their frequent texts, Ivy learns that Jason's mother, Margaret, has become a bit of a "mystic woo-woo nutcase". (His words, not hers! And clearly said with love.) This, apparently, has been an evolution over time, she was not so spiritual when he and his sister were kids.

Jason will periodically text Ivy with some of his mom's quotes and theories. One surprising revelation is that his mom is loyal to a certain celebrity and her factless beauty cult, so the idea of jade eggs and purposely getting stung by bees comes up on various occasions. Jason also lets Ivy know that, in case she hadn't heard, his mom says that wearing underwire bras cause breast cancer. "So, beware."

JASON
I'm just saying, if you're super attached to your breasts, you're going to want to keep underwires far away from them!

IVY
I AM quite attached to them

JASON
Understandable

IVY
Sports bra it is!
Or maybe it's safest to just go braless
Bras are uncomfortable anyway
I'll just let them hang free to be on the safe side. Best not to risk it

JASON

IVY
Does this mean your mom has been
wandering around without a bra?

JASON
Let's not talk about my mom's breasts

IVY
Oh sure, THAT would be inappropriate

Jason chuckles and decides not to reply since all he can think about now are Ivy's breasts. Putting his phone down, he has a distinct wave of emotion. He misses Ivy. Their sleepover felt truly comfortable. He didn't think he could sleep so well next to someone new.

In some ways, this distance is probably good. It's given him a chance to step back and evaluate things. On his drive, he considered a real, romantic relationship with Ivy and for that moment, he was happy. It just felt … right. He continues to have spicy dreams about her, and he thinks about touching her a lot more than someone should think about touching a friend. He has no problem seeing himself with her for the rest of his life and the idea is somehow both soothing and terrifying.

Then he remembers how happy he was with Nicole, how sure he was that their relationship was solid, and how their demise came out of nowhere. It completely destroyed him. He can't handle that again.

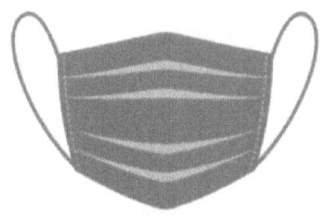

<u>CHAPTER 23</u>

Ivy sends thanks to the parking gods that she was able to find a spot outside her building since the two-block hike she usually deals with would be a challenge with this haul of heavy grocery bags. She's always been one of those people who likes to make the fewest trips to the car as possible. As she packs three bags full of canned goods onto one shoulder and starts to wonder if she can actually handle this, she hears Otto shout out to her.

"Do you need a hand there?"

Ivy looks up to see Otto and Hildy coming out of their building and gives him an acknowledging head bop. "I think I've got it, thank you though."

But Otto has already started to cross the street toward her, gesturing for her to give him one of the bags, Hildy following at his heels. Ivy considers making a more declarative declination, but the bags are heavy, and Otto does have a mask on, so she concedes.

"Thank you," she says begrudgingly. "I wasn't really thinking about getting everything inside when I stocked up on canned goods."

"I understand," Otto says as he takes a bag on each shoulder. "Hildy's food was on sale the other day and you'd better believe I grabbed extras. Luckily for me, I've got my grocery cart so it's only a pain when I get to my front stairs."

Ivy leads the way into her building, trying her best to keep some distance from Otto just to be on the safe side. He and Hildy follow Ivy to her apartment door.

"You can just leave those here. Thank you for your help. I appreciate it."

Otto sets the bags down in the hall as Hildy sniffs at the neighbor's front door. "No problem. I haven't been in this building in forever. It's fun to be back inside."

"Oh, yah? Does the hall look the same as you remember?" Ivy asks.

"Yah, not too much has changed. I used to live on the top floor. Just for a year or two until I found my place across the street. I've been there for about twenty years now."

"Really?" Is this how he and Annie know each other? Ivy wonders how long Annie has been in the building. As if reading her mind, Otto comments.

"Yep. At that time, Annie lived downstairs and Milt, the guy who feeds the birds in the park, he lived here too. Not too many of us still around. But I love this area."

"I didn't realize you guys had been here that long."

"Oh yah. Actually, at that time, Annie was the building manager and Milt left because he used to feel the birds and squirrels out front, and she told him he couldn't do that anymore because it would cause an infestation. He found a place a block or two over."

"Interesting," Ivy says, sincerely. "Well, thank you for the help and the fun neighborhood history."

"Any time. I've got loads of stories."

"Why is that dog in here and not on a leash?" rings out from down the hall, near the lobby where Annie stands with her hands on her hips.

"Otto helped me bring in my groceries," Ivy shouts back, with a little extra friendliness to help smooth things over.

"We were just leaving," Otto says as he heads toward Annie and the exit. "Come on, Hildy."

Annie stands her ground, despite partially blocking the exit, just watching as Otto and Hildy make their way toward her. Ivy can hear Annie say something to him, at a much lower tone. Something like, "You know it's illegal to have your dog off leash."

Ivy hears Otto reply, "Have a good day, Annie." Ivy is tempted to see if they say anything else, but she's also afraid if she lingers outside her door too long, Annie might try to talk to her. So, she opens her door and plops the bags inside before closing the door behind her, doing her best to listen for any fighting. But it seems that Otto was able to escape the building safely.

After she puts away her groceries, Ivy texts Jason.

> IVY
> My theory that Annie and Otto are former lovers might not be correct. Turns out, Annie used to be the building manager here and Otto used to live on the top floor.

JASON
They could still have had a sexy building affair that ended poorly

> IVY
> True, but I think it was more about Annie being a mean manager
> If you're trying to escape a lover, go further than the building across the street!

JASON
Good point
You're gonna solve this mystery soon, I can
feel it

IVY
I think we need to double team them

JASON
Excuse me

IVY
You're going to need to casually get
some info from one or both of them

JASON
The very first thing I do when I get home will
be to track them both down and interrogate
them

IVY
Thank you. That's all I ask of you

JASON
Totally reasonable

IVY
A worthy use of your time

Jason hears his mother coming and quickly puts his phone down, making sure his typical Ivy-induced smile is off his face. Margaret has been trying to not so subtly delve into his dating life, reminding him it has been over a year since his divorce was finalized. He needs to move on. Jason knows that she means well, but her constant comments about how it's "not too late" for him to have a family irritate him so much it is nearly physical, like bugs crawling on his skin.

Every time she begins to move the conversation toward his love life, he will say something particularly outlandish to distract her. Perhaps claiming that capitalism has saved the United States from spiraling into a communist hellscape. Or declaring that global warming can't be real, after all, it was nice and cool all night! It's worked so far, but he is a little concerned about her blood pressure.

Despite her near daily attempts to warn him that he is on the path to die alone, Jason is glad he visited and was able to help his mom and stepdad out. It was particularly difficult for Margaret since hospital visits are restricted with COVID-19 and she has not been separated from Bill for more than a day in the 35 years they've been married.

Jason stays long enough to be sure both his mom and Bill are settled in and doing well and able to be on their own before he heads back to Los Angeles. Unfortunately, his mom takes this last day of his visit as her very last chance to get through to him, so she goes hard.

"Honey, I really need to talk to you," she says, gesturing for him to sit down at the kitchen table with her.

"What's up, mom?"

"I know you want to avoid talking about this, but I really am worried about you," Margaret continues, determined to get this out. "I understand that you aren't ready for a relationship yet, but I want to make sure you haven't decided you never want another relationship ever again."

Jason understands he can't avoid this any longer. "What if I have decided that?"

"It's just not healthy, honey. You're only in your forties. I know that seems old to you right now, but you have a lot of life still left to live and I don't want to see you do it alone just because you're scared."

"I don't think being alone is so bad," Jason says. He and his mom both know he's lying.

"Honey, I'm not saying being alone is bad for everyone. But it's bad for *you*. You and Nicole had a wonderful relationship. I know you're mad I still talk to her, but don't think I didn't tell her how badly she really fucked up when she cheated on you."

"Mom!" Jason scolds in exaggerated shock at her foul language.

Margaret ignores him, determined to not let him distract her again. "I know she made a mistake. She knows she made a mistake in how she handled things. And I know why you couldn't make things work. But she's moved on to a new husband and baby and you're just lost."

"Mom, it's not the same. We didn't leave our marriage on even footing. I was the one damaged by her betrayal. Also, it's not a great time to date. Remember how there's a pandemic going on? How would I even find anyone?" Jason is so thankful he hasn't told his family about Ivy; it makes it much easier to blame the pandemic than to admit his mom is right and he is scared.

"I loved your father very much. And he loved me. And believe it or not, he loved you and Angie too. He just wasn't meant to be a father. His family pressured him to settle down, but he didn't really want kids and I think we both knew it and we both ignored it. I was left with two kids and a broken heart when he left. But not too much later, I met Bill. And I let myself be open to new love. You can love more than once, especially if you're honest about what you want and what you have to offer."

Jason takes this in but doesn't say anything. He chooses not to point out that she is pressuring him just like his father's family pressured his father and, as she just said, it did not work out. But as Jason debates whether it's worth trying to argue with her, Bill enters the kitchen.

"Margaret, leave him alone. He will move on when he's ready." Then Jason and Bill exchange a quick but familiar conspiratorial smile.

Now that she's outnumbered and has gotten her point across, Margaret surrenders. "Fine," she says, looking at Jason, "I love you. I want you to be happy. Please just think about what I said. I'm your mother, I want what's best for you and I know when you're lying. Even when you're lying to yourself." She gets up from the table and before leaving the kitchen, she looks back at Jason. "I bought you some aluminum-free deodorant. The stuff you have is going to give you cancer."

Classic Margaret.

CHAPTER 24

Jason arrives back to his apartment late at night, having decided to enjoy a nice nighttime drive back home, indulging in a solo hootenanny for as long as his voice can handle. It really is a great stress-reliever. It's difficult to obsess over things when you are belting out "Knock Three Times" by Tony Orlando and Dawn.

He texts Ivy in the morning letting her know he's back, but that he wants to isolate for two weeks before seeing her, just to be on the safe side. Ivy appreciates his caution, and they plan for dinner and Gilmore Girls two weeks from today.

Until then, Ivy continues her daily routine which now includes the occasional trip to her local coffee shops, justifying the expense and risk of exposure by telling herself that she is supporting small businesses and helping the economy. She drives to get her very favorite latte from Jameson and grabs a second one which, upon her return, she places outside of Jason's door.

> IVY
> I left you a latte outside your door
> Along with some pastry that has cream
> cheese and bacon, so even though I
> haven't tried it, how bad could it be?
> They're from the place I told you about
> Enjoy!

JASON
You are wonderful
I'm so sick of my instant coffee
Thank you

Jason texts again a few minutes later

JASON
These are both really good.
I can't place the flavor of the latte, what is it?

IVY
Lavender!
Who would have thought, right?

JASON
Why is that so LA to me?

IVY
I don't know. But it totally is.

After finishing his latte and delicious pastry, Jason begins a morning of back-to-back meetings to coordinate his newest project. It is by far his least favorite part of his job. On his first real break between meetings, he takes the opportunity to shower. He lets the hot water run over him for a bit, letting his tense muscles relax. He surveys his recently stocked shelf full of bottles, jars, and bars and reaches for his favorite shampoo.

Many years ago, Nicole drilled into his brain the importance of taking care of his skin and indulging in selfcare. She didn't call it that at the time, of course, but she always understood the importance of investing in your mental health. She used to come home with a shopping bag or two, saying "Treat yo' self" just like Tom and Donna from Parks and Rec as she handed him the products she thought he would like. Jason's been lazy about these little luxuries for a while now. But since spending time with Ivy, and smelling her light clean scent, he was inspired to go online and splurge on all his old favorites.

As he begins to lather and massage his scalp, he recalls a conversation he overheard at work a few years back as he waited for his coffee at the breakroom machine. One of the young single guys in the office was saying he used one product for everything: facewash, shampoo, body wash, all from one bottle and the women in the break room immediately began to advise him on products he should consider instead.

The women were not judgmental, not really. Mostly, they had just wanted to help this obviously clueless guy out. They wanted him to have healthy skin, so they were sharing their knowledge with him, and the kid seemed to be receptive to their suggestions.

Then, another coworker, an older man, interrupted to tell the young guy to ignore the women, basically dismissing all their recommendations as mindless feminine chatter. Jason remembers thinking to himself at the time that the older man really should have paid attention to what the women were saying because his skin looked like powdered leather.

He didn't fully understand at the time, but he so clearly sees now how dismissive that was of the older man. The kid didn't appear offended or in need of rescue. The older guy clearly just thought that men don't need beauty products, those things are "girly". Jason wonders if he would have ever noticed the deeper implications of the older man's actions if he had not spent so much time with Ivy recently.

She looks at things so differently than he does, simply by virtue of coming from different life experiences, and even when he doesn't fully agree with her take on a topic or situation, he is still made aware that his view is not necessarily the only one.

Jason also considers that the older guy who thought the women discussing skincare was nothing but mindless chatter was the same guy who routinely spent hours of the workday discussing sports and Game of Thrones with other male workers, and somehow that was a good use of his time.

Lost in thought, Jason is brought back to the present when he notices something. He looks down to see that, among the thick suds of moisturizing soap, there is a long blond hair wrapped around the head of his penis. He has found a few of Ivy's hairs in unexpected places. Once he found one in his bed, even though she has not been in his apartment since their sterile hug. Another time, he found one in his shoe, but he had been walking around her apartment in his socks, so that did make sense. But this? How the hell did it not only get through his pants and underwear but also manage to lovingly hug his penis? He unwinds the hair and considers texting Ivy about this, but decides to keep this to himself, intuiting that perhaps that would cross the line of their candid sharing, for now.

***

Their reunion dinner is all planned. Ivy orders from a new place (well, new to her) that she tried while Jason was away and thought he would really like. When she tells him she's planning on picking it up given the outrageous delivery fee, he offers to join her.

"Where did you order from?" Jason asks.

"I always get the name wrong, it's something like Good Down Home Southern."

"Down Home Southern Café?" Jason asks.

"Yes!"

"Where did you get 'good' from?" he asks with an easy chuckle.

"I don't know!" Ivy replies, mock exasperation in her tone. "But now it's in my head and I'll never get the damn name right again! Have you eaten there before?"

"Uh, yes. I used to eat there pretty often. With my ex-wife."

"Oh. Do you not want to eat there? We can pick up some other food and I'll save this for later."

"No, it's fine," says Jason. "They do have good food. It was Nicole's favorite so it was a regular spot for us." He continues with exaggerated bravery. "I can *probably* avoid thinking about her with every single bite of delicious food I take."

Ivy looks over at him with a sheepish smile and he winks back to assure her he's fine.

They don't say anything else until they arrive at the restaurant where Ivy makes a couple of fruitless loops around the block looking for parking, but her bladder makes her choose a not exactly legal spot to stop.

"I always thought weak bladders were a mom thing, not just an aging woman thing," Ivy complains as she puts the car in park, puts her hazards on, and unbuckles her seatbelt. "Be right back!"

She runs in to get the order while Jason stays with the car in case parking enforcement drives by. A little after she enters the restaurant, she sends him a text.

IVY
There was an issue with our order so it isn't ready
They claim it will only be five minutes though

JASON
No problem
I was arrested and the car was towed
But no rush

                              IVY
                              Oh cool, I can take my sweet time then

With time to kill, Jason checks his email. He has a message from his mom who has forwarded him an invitation with a message saying, "Consider sending a gift. It would be a nice gesture." It's an invitation for a Zoom event, 'Hunter and Nicole's Baby Sprinkle' and his heart drops. He's not even entirely sure what the event is, that combination of words making no sense to him, but his mom's note makes it clear that Nicole is having another baby.

He looks at the details of date, time, and instructions that gifts are not necessary, but they are registered at a few places and presents can be shipped directly to the family's home. As he reads the last two words, he pictures the condo he and Nicole lived in, now full of toys and another man's clothes and he starts to feel what is becoming a familiar unpleasant sensation in his chest.

When he glances up from his phone, remembering he is supposed to be on the lookout for parking enforcement, Jason sees a couple walking down the sidewalk toward the restaurant. The man is tall and muscular and has his hair perfectly styled, he holds the hand of a thin woman with short hair carrying a child who looks to be nearly too big for the woman to manage. The couple's faces are covered by their masks, but having just seen that email, he's sure it's Nicole, her new husband and their daughter. Jason freezes, unable to look away from them, watching them until they enter the restaurant.

A moment later, he realizes he's not breathing, and a wave of nausea passes through him. He's processing these feelings as Ivy opens the door and puts a large bag of food in the backseat.

"Hooray, we weren't really towed! This food smells amazing, well worth the wait," she says as she gets into the car. Her tone changes when she sees Jason's stricken face and asks, "Are you okay?"

Jason manages to nod and between the deep breaths he has started to take, he ekes out, "Just forgot to breathe."

Ivy nods, but notices that his attempts to breathe deeply don't seem to be helping him. "Is this a panic attack?" she asks, and he nods his head in reply. "Got it. I've had those before along with stress gags. Can I do anything for you?"

Jason shakes his head this time and manages to say, "You can drive. I'll be fine."

"Okay then, let's head back home. Just let me know if you need anything," she says. Jason replies by giving her a thumbs up.

Seeing the sweat on his forehead, she turns all the AC vents toward him, then rolls down a window for some fresh air as she checks her mirrors to make sure the coast is clear.

Ivy pulls away from the curb and Jason glances out the window to see the same couple and their baby coming back out of the restaurant, the man now holding the chubby baby and the woman carrying their takeout order. He can clearly see now that the woman barely resembles Nicole and, small detail, is not pregnant! The lingering tightness in his chest loosens its grip.

When they get back to their building, Ivy offers Jason an out, asking if he wants to skip dinner and go take a nap or something. He appreciates the offer but declines. They go back to her place and Ivy makes the executive decision that they should eat at the coffee table so they can start the show and Jason won't feel like he needs to talk. They watch two full episodes before Ivy decides to broach the subject.

"Do you want to talk about it? Would that help?" Ivy asks.

Jason takes a moment to answer. "My mom forwarded me an email for my ex-wife's baby shower, I think. Or something like that. And it shouldn't bother me, she already has a kid with her new husband. But something hit me and then I thought I saw them, a little happy family, and I felt my blood go cold with this sense of dread and couldn't breathe."

"A Dementor attack. I knew it," Ivy says with a smile. And Jason smiles back. "Did you and Nicole want kids?" she asks gently and while it could be considered by some to be an insensitive question, Ivy somehow knows it's not.

"No!" Jason says, his unresolved confusion at the situation becoming evident. "We talked about it a lot in our twenties and we both agreed we didn't want kids. We also discussed it again in our thirties and decided we still didn't. Then, after she told me about the affair and we were trying to work things out, she found out she was pregnant. With *his* child. And all of a sudden, she couldn't wait to be a mom! And the fucked up thing is, I still wasn't ready to give up on us and while I was trying to decide if I could handle raising another man's child with my wife, she made the decision for me by leaving me."

"I'm so sorry," Ivy replies with genuine sympathy.

"And I don't begrudge her a family if she wants one. But she *didn't* want one. Or maybe she just didn't want one with me," he says, unable to stop himself. "I don't know if she changed her mind and just never told me or changed her mind when she found out she was pregnant or what happened! But one day we were a happily married couple, I thought, and then the next day, she was the mother of a child that's not mine."

Ivy places her hand on his leg and then considers that he may not want to be touched right now, but before she can remove it, he places his hand on hers, almost unconsciously as he continues ranting.

"And I can't even fathom why my mom sent me that email. She wants me to move on and find a new wife or girlfriend or something, but I think she gets confused about what's motivation and what's just cruel."

Jason continues to purge these buried grievances, sharing details about his divorce and how ugly it got, how angry he got, how it dragged on for longer than was healthy for anyone. He shares everything he's been keeping inside for so long as Ivy listens attentively.

Rant eventually winding down, Jason wraps up with a deep breath and a slight smirk. "I think that's what everyone has been warning me about, why I shouldn't ignore my feelings."

"It's like an emotional volcano," Ivy says, smiling back at him.

"Sorry I erupted all over you."

Ivy laughs, "I wouldn't have referred to it that way, but I'm glad you shared. I hope you feel better."

"I do feel better," and he continues dryly, "Shooting my hot, molten, emotional lava all over you."

"Oh my god, no. You mustn't." Ivy says as she puts a hand over Jason's mouth.

She feels his smile under her palm, and she smiles back before taking her hand away. Toby comes into the room, sitting next to them on the floor and staring at them to make it clear that he has noticed that his walk is overdue.

Ivy and Jason take Toby out together and as they go down the hallway, they pass an apartment with a large jar of peanut butter sitting outside the door. Jason and Ivy look at each other and don't say anything, but the looks they share both say, "What the fuck?"

Coming back in from their walk, Jason decides he should go to bed. Up to his lonely, sad bed. They pause at the stairs and Jason pulls down his mask to quickly kiss Ivy on her forehead, as he has done before. But as she tells him good night and he looks in her eyes, a rush of warmth runs through him. Instead of a friendly peck, he removes the loop of her mask from her ear, letting one side of her mask fall and leans in to kiss her full on the mouth.

Ivy tenses for a second, first surprised by the removal of her mask, then by the kiss itself. But after a moment, she leans into it. Something about it takes her back in time, to her first kiss with her first real boyfriend, before she had ever been hurt by love and she had nothing but hope and trust in romance. Before anyone had ever treated her badly or made her feel like she wasn't good enough. It feels natural. And wonderful.

The warmth spreading through her body is pure and somehow peaceful and completely out of proportion to the innocent kiss she is experiencing right now. She feels so clearly that it's not really the kiss itself causing this feeling as much as it's the person she's kissing.

As Jason moves closer, moving his hand to her hip, they are interrupted by the sound of the door to apartment six opening. They turn their heads and make eye contact with the woman who is reaching down to grab the massive jar of peanut butter. There is a moment when nobody is sure who should be more embarrassed and then Apartment Six retreats into her apartment, jar in hand.

Jason and Ivy make eye contact and wordlessly share a look that, once again, communicates the weirdness of what just happened. Then there's an awkward pause before Jason begins to speak, an apology on his lips, but Ivy interrupts him.

"It's okay, I know you were upset before. You just…" and she trails off, her excuse for him not fully fleshed out, just knowing he didn't mean it.

"I'm not upset anymore, I just really wanted to do that. But I shouldn't have. I'm sorry." He kisses her on the forehead and heads upstairs with a quick, "Good night."

Ivy goes back to her apartment, confused. And if she's being honest, a little turned-on. And maybe pissed. There's a lot going on for her emotionally right now. That was the beginning of a very nice kiss. Fucking Apartment Six! What kinky-ass shit was she up to anyway with that much peanut butter?

Ivy feels like she should text Jason so there isn't any weirdness when they see each other next, but she's not sure what to say so she proceeds with her nightly bedtime ritual and climbs into bed, doing her best to not obsess over what that kiss meant.

Meanwhile, Jason is pacing his apartment, knowing he shouldn't have left Ivy like that, but not really clear what he should have said or done. Or what he should say now. Or maybe what he should text? After debating a while about what to do for damage control, he texts Ivy. It's late, she could be asleep, but if she is, she'll have silenced her phone. He takes his time finding the right words.

JASON
I'm sorry. You mean a lot to me and I should
not have done that. As you saw earlier, I still
have a lot of shit to work out and am
obviously not ready for a relationship right
now. I crossed a line.

Ivy is awake and playing Sudoku on her phone, so when his message comes through, she sees it immediately. She considers replying, but unsure of what she wants to say, she puts her phone on her nightstand, and rolls to her side to go to sleep.

In the morning, Ivy takes some time to obsess over what she wants to write back. For a man who claims to be bad at expressing his emotions, she appreciates that Jason is always willing to calmly address things when necessary. It displays a maturity that she herself lacks. Her tendency is to joke and deflect when awkward topics come around. So rather than sending something like, "Good morning, mouth rapist!" which is her first inclination, she decides to match Jason's sincerity.

> IVY
> I understand. You mean a lot to me too

And then, unable to be *too* serious, she sends another text.

> IVY
> And not just because of your amazing lasagna and brownies

A little while later, Jason replies. Much earlier than Ivy expected him to be awake.

JASON
I really like you and even though we haven't known each other that long, you've become a very important person in my life
I really enjoy spending time with you and I hope I didn't ruin anything

Reading his text, Ivy's eyes begin to water. There he goes again, Ivy thinks. Being sweet.

          IVY
          I appreciate that
          And I also enjoy spending time with you
          You did not ruin our friendship
          I agree that this is not a good time for
          us to be more than friends
          So no more kissing

JASON
Agreed
Wanna fuck?

          IVY
          <laughing emoji>
          Yah, that's totally fine
          Just no kissing

     JASON AND IVY
     Pretty Woman rules

     JASON AND IVY
     Jinx!

          IVY
          Quick, what number am I thinking of?

JASON
69

IVY
3
I guess we aren't psychic
But you're a perv

JASON
Guilty as charged

IVY
You wanna GG and dinner on Saturday?

JASON
Is that your version of Netflix and chill?

IVY
Yes
The not sexy, just friends, version

JASON
Yes, I want to GG&D
6PM?

IVY
<thumbs up emoji>
See you Saturday

CHAPTER 25

It's Friday night and the long-awaited new season of Great British Baking Show has premiered. Holly has some strong feelings.

"Well, this season is going to blow!" she says.

"Maybe it gets better. You know, like life for gay teens," replies Ivy.

"I hate the new host. And I didn't love the old one, so not great!"

"It doesn't work to have two weird hosts. You need a straight man. Unlike a gay teen," Ivy says.

"This sucks. I think we're looking at the best British amateur bakers-who also had no commitments and could quarantine for a month. Really cuts down on the talent, apparently."

The two sisters continue to discuss Great British Baking Show, offering critiques on this new season and past seasons as well. They continue to chat about a dozen different topics for the next hour before Holly brings the conversation around to Jason.

"So, how's your boyfriend?" she asks in that teasing older sister tone.

"Well, I don't have a boyfriend, so I don't know to whom you are referring. But if you mean my *friend* Jason, he's good."

"Did you ever figure out what he does for a living?" Holly asks.

"Kind of, he develops apps or something. But nothing fun, just stuff for companies. Like scheduling or customer service or shopping apps, I think. We both agreed our jobs are too boring to discuss. We complain about co-workers and shit, but we don't really discuss the details of our actual work."

"Oh, then has he always worked from home?"

"I don't think so. But he definitely doesn't go into any office now. And I get the impression he's in charge of how many hours he works," Ivy says.

"Must be nice. Have you two moved in together yet?"

"Stop it! We don't even see each other that often!" Ivy says in that teased younger sister tone. "He walks with Toby and I a couple of days a week and then we usually will hang out once or twice during the weekend."

"Oh yah, you barely see him. Let me ask you this. Does he have a key to your place?" Ivy's lack of response answers for her. "I knew it."

"He only has it because I had to go into the office a few times and Toby has gotten used to our new schedule, so Jason walked him for me," Ivy replies.

"Okay, so you trust him with your key *and* Toby? That's true love right there."

"Look, at another time, I'd happily date him. He's cool and we get along well. But we are just friends right now," Ivy says with a tone that Holly knows means she is getting dangerously close to crossing the line from tolerantly playful into pissy, so she changes the subject.

"If you can tear yourself away from your *friend*, I still think you and Toby should visit me for Thanksgiving. Or hell, bring Jason with you!" Holly says.

"That would probably be fun, actually. I think you'd like him."

"It's up to you, he can come if you want," Holly says.

"I'm thinking about it. Well, thinking about visiting, I don't know about the inviting Jason part. Might be too weird to suggest he meet my family. But I'm up for driving there so I can avoid plane germs and so Toby can come, but I don't know if it's safe to stay in hotels right now. I'd probably need to stay the night in Utah. Does Utah even believe in COVID?"

"Probably not, but I think just from legal liability, the hotel will take the recommended precautions," Holly replies.

"How are we already discussing Thanksgiving? This year has been so weird. I feel like we've been in this shit for a decade but then I'm also surprised it's September. It makes no sense," Ivy says.

"I think the isolation and monotony fuck with you," Holly agrees.

"Oh my god," Ivy says, changing the subject, "Did I tell you about the hand cream I found that has cured my sad, cracked, over-washed hands?" And Jason is not mentioned again on this call.

***

The following night, Ivy and Jason sit at the coffee table, their plates of grilled vegetables and chicken breasts in front of them. Ivy starts the show and during the opening theme, Jason stops singing along for a moment to issue a warning.

"Now I know I warned you about season seven, which is going to suck. But I forgot about another dark spot in the series."

"Oh no, does Luke die?" Ivy asks.

"What? No. Why would you say that?"

In response, Ivy raises her shoulders and makes that noise that clearly means, "I don't know," but without actually saying the words.

"Spoiler, but Luke remains alive throughout the series. No, I'm afraid there's a character misstep here in season four. And it pains me to say this, but you are about to meet Jason. And Jason is terrible. He is Lorelei's worst boyfriend, by far."

"But all the Jasons I know are so cool," Ivy says with a cheeky smile.

"I know, we're usually awesome. But not this one. He really let all of us Jasons down. Please do your best to forgive them for this error in writing and accept he's going to be with us for a while."

"Until *he* dies?"

"No! Nobody dies!"

"You didn't say spoiler!" Ivy teases.

After they finish their dinner, Ivy takes their empty plates to the kitchen and, a few minutes later, returns with dessert. She sets down a tray that has two small glasses of milk and a plate with a stack of homemade peanut butter cookies neatly arranged.

She slides the tray in front of Jason, giving him a knowing glance. She waits to see if he notices the cookies, which he does, casually saying, "Oh, do you also have a jumbo jar of peanut butter or was this borrowed from Apartment Six?"

"Borrowed. I figured she had enough to share. Her dog sure was giving me dirty looks though."

They enjoy their milk and cookies and continue the show. After a couple of episodes, they move to their designated spots on the couch and this comfort and familiarity keeps them happily marathoning for hours, only interrupted for occasional conversational tangents, Toby's evening walk, trips to the bathroom, and drink refills.

Several episodes in, Ivy readjusts to move her small pillow to the arm of the couch, lying down, and pulling her legs in. In this position she's not touching Jason, but she is still clearly violating the established boundaries of the couch.

Observing this encroachment, Jason also readjusts. But instead of moving his pillow to his arm of the couch, placing them foot to foot, he puts his pillow on Ivy's hip and snuggles up to her, essentially spooning her legs. He then takes his Snuggie and places it as much over both of them as he can manage. Ivy is a little surprised by this, having assumed he was going to keep his distance after their kiss, but she's not complaining.

Hours later, their comfortable silence is broken when Ivy comments on the episode in which Lorelei first sees Jason's apartment and learns that he cannot sleep with anyone in his room with him, so he escorts her to a special guest bedroom set up just for his ladies.

"Obviously, Jason is a charmless weirdo," Ivy says, "buuuut I like this separate bedrooms idea. It makes sense to me."

"Really? You'd be fine if you had sex with a man and then he escorted you out of his room?"

"No, it's weird and off-putting on a date. For one night, you just have to accept you're not going to sleep and let the person stay with you. But long term, I get it. If you had rules with it, I think it could work."

"Bedroom rules? Sounds romantic," Jason laughs.

"It could be! Cute rules like sleepovers in either room are always welcome, barring someone being sick or having to get up early or something. There would be an open-door policy."

"Then why not just have one room?" Jason asks.

"Because sometimes it's nice to be alone, you know? Especially if one person snores. Or let's say you're super gassy one evening, you don't have to be self-conscious about being a terrible fart monster all night. And then your partner doesn't have to spend a night being a victim of a terrible fart monster. Everyone wins."

"Is continuous farting something you're concerned about? Should I move?" Jason asks, sitting up a bit to give her an exaggerated look and distance himself from her butt.

"No, you're fine," Ivy says, and she gestures for him to put his head back down, to assure him he should stay where he is. "For now, at least."

"Please give me plenty of warning if things change."

"But also," Ivy continues, "Sometimes people have different schedules. Someone might routinely get up several hours before the other person or go to bed hours after the other person. Or like the room to be different temperatures. That's not a problem in separate rooms."

"But then you lose the intimacy of sleeping next to someone every night. To let someone hear you snore or know you farted all night long and not hold it against you is letting down your guard. That's where intimacy comes from," Jason says.

"You can still have intimacy in the relationship. And you *can* spend the night together, it's just not necessarily *every* night. If you think about it, it would make the nights that you choose to share a bedroom even more special," Ivy says.

"I don't know. Still seems odd to me."

"It's non-traditional for sure, I'm just saying I think it's practical and probably prevents some resentments."

"Maybe," he half-heartedly replies.

Ivy, noting the lack of earnestness in his response, presses on. "You said you like having your own bathroom, right?"

"Yes."

"Well, would you consider having a primary suite with his and hers bathrooms?"

"'Primary' suite?" Jason asks.

"Yes, we're not supposed to use the term 'master' anymore. I just learned that on TikTok."

"Oh. I never even thought about that. Glad the younger generations are teaching us something."

"So, would you like his and hers bathrooms?" she asks again.

"Yes. Obviously. That would be heaven."

"You would lose intimacy with that too. Letting someone see you get ready or letting someone smell your shit is also letting your guard down," Ivy says, feeling she is really nailing this argument.

Jason thinks this over. "I guess. Maybe I'm just old-fashioned."

"And maybe I've just lived alone too long, but I would say most of the times I've stayed at a man's place, or he stayed with me, we didn't sleep well. It's possible that if we lived together, we would have finally gotten used to each other. But I think separate bedrooms are practical. I think I might have to alter my dream home plans to include two upstairs suites and if I'm not with someone when I win the lottery, Toby will get his own room."

"Honestly, I'm surprised Toby having his own room wasn't part of your plan to begin with," Jason teases. "I see your point about the rooms. But I think I just love cuddling too much to think of separate beds."

"Oh my god, that's adorable. You win."

"I know," Jason grunts. "I'm so fucking charming."

They finish the episode and decide to call it a night. As Jason helps collect any random items and take the tray back into the kitchen, he begins to make plans for their next hang out.

"I was thinking of doing something special for dinner next weekend. Wanna join me?" he asks.

"Sure, what's the occasion?"

"Oh, nothing special. It's my fortynnmmm birthday," Jason says, purposely mumbling through his exact age.

"Your birthday? Oh, then I'm definitely in. And I can treat!" Ivy says enthusiastically.

"Oh no, I want to get some stupidly expensive food. And then order a dumb amount of it. Like, I should be ashamed of myself kind of a meal, so I'll pay. Your company will be gift enough for me," Jason assures her.

"Awwwww, you're goddamn right it is."

"When's *your* birthday?" he asks, causally.

"Oh," Ivy replies somewhat bashfully, "It was in May."

"What?! Why didn't you say anything?"

"Well, it was a particularly rough time, and I didn't need a celebration or anything so it didn't seem worth mentioning."

Jason smiles at her and says, "Then consider this ridiculously expensive dinner a joint birthday party!"

"I'm excited!" Ivy says.

CHAPTER 26

Jason and Ivy decide to take their celebration to the park, not just to shake things up a bit, but because this meal requires a larger eating space. Jason ordered from a local restaurant without knowing it just so happens to be one of Ivy's favorites, her default fancy dinner celebration location. Carrying way too many bags for a meal for two, they score the best picnic table in the park, the one farthest from the park's main path.

Ivy wipes everything down before covering the table with a disposable bright yellow tablecloth she found in her pantry, unopened, from some past occasion she can't even remember. She also made a cute fake birthday cake centerpiece from craft paper for the occasion and brought a few mason jars filled with aquarium rocks and tealights as weights for the tablecloth. It's not her most beautiful table-scape, but it earns high praise from Jason and it adds to the festive vibe.

They begin the meal with a couple of shared appetizers. Each bite Ivy takes inspires her little happy dance, which Jason does not participate in but, as always, thoroughly enjoys watching. They move onto their salads and then devour their conservatively portioned steaks with baked potato and braised red cabbage. At that point, they reluctantly set aside their desserts, their jeans painfully garroting their full stomachs.

"The one bad part of eating at the park is not being able to wear pajama pants," Ivy comments, letting out a deep breath.

They continue to chat while waiting for motivation to get up and waddle home when Otto and Hildy come through the park on their evening stroll. Otto makes his way over, Hildy casually following a few feet behind.

"Let the interrogation begin," Jason whispers to Ivy as the two of them put their masks back on. Ivy giggles back.

"Hey you two!" Otto says as he stops a few feet from their table. "Look at all this! What are you celebrating?"

Ivy thinks she sees Jason shoot her a look, warning her not to tell Otto it's his birthday, but she can't help herself. "It's Jason's birthday!" she says, and it's clear to Jason that she has a shit-eating grin under her mask.

"Well, happy birthday!" Otto says with enthusiasm. "This looks like a great way to celebrate."

"It was a very good birthday meal," Jason replies. "But it's actually a joint birthday dinner, we missed Ivy's birthday in May." Ivy's pretty sure she hears him emphasizing the month to make sure if Otto knows his birthday, he also knows hers.

"That's nice. Well, I don't want to interrupt you two," Otto says as he turns to look for Hildy.

"You're not interrupting, we just hadn't gotten the energy to pack up and head home. Would you like some?" Jason says gesturing to an open container.

Otto happily accepts the extra bread and cheese from the appetizer they didn't finish and hadn't boxed back up yet. Ivy can tell Otto is happy to see her and Jason together, she even thinks she sees him wink at her when he leaves.

"Your interrogation skills need work," Ivy says to Jason once Otto is out of earshot.

"Really? I thought I was about to make him crack."

"One more offer of delicious food and you would have had him spilling his guts," she teases.

When the mosquitos start to get particularly aggressive, Jason and Ivy pack up their leftovers, clean up their decorations, and head back home. They agree that a nice walk might be the best way to help digest the generous amount of food they've eaten, but not wanting to deal with Toby's frequent stops, they decide to walk without him.

They take the leftovers to Jason's apartment, so they don't give Toby the false hope of them sticking around. Ivy waits in Jason's quarantine zone, so she does not have to remove her shoes. She's not sure if bending over to untie her laces would be an option right now, she's so full. As Jason takes the food to his kitchen, Ivy looks around his bleak apartment.

"You've really made a lot of progress with your decorating," she says, sarcastically.

"Hey! I *have* made a lot of progress," Jason replies as he comes out of the kitchen and walks into his living room. "Not only do I have my Gryffindor Snuggie, but I have this!" He grabs a coaster from his end table and holds it up proudly.

"I'm sorry, is that one of the paper coasters that came with our Good Home Down Southern order?" Ivy asks, smiling.

"Down Home Southern Café?"

"Yah, I'm pretty sure that's what I said."

"It *is* from there," Jason confirms. "But I thought to bring it home and place it on my table. That's initiative. That's decorating!" Jason brags.

"Very impressive. It really adds something to the place. Good job."

"I'm going to grab a jacket, do you need one?" Jason asks, as he goes into his room.

"Thanks, but I doubt any of your jackets will fit me."

"Excuse me, I am not some dainty little boy, madam. You must not have noticed my super manly, wide, linebacker shoulders. I'm sure I have something that will work for you, if you want one."

Ivy decides not to comment on his broad shoulders and back, something she has indeed noticed and has always enjoyed. "Fine, then yes. That'd be nice. I will take an extra large linebacker hoodie from you."

Jason comes out in his go-to comfy hoodie that Ivy has seen a dozen times before and hands her another hoodie. It's very soft and, slipping it on over her head, is relieved to see that it does in fact fit. It's a little tight through the butt and hip area, but not enough that she's going to stretch it out or anything.

"See?" Jason says, "Beautiful."

Ivy is grateful she put her mask back on so quickly, but to make sure she's definitely hidden her blushing reaction she says, with faux confidence, "I know. I look amazing in hoodies. I can't help it."

They decide to take a route that they haven't taken in a while, mainly due to Toby's obsession with a certain flowering bush that he always wants to stop and sniff but which is often swarming with bees, which he is allergic to. But without Toby, they take advantage of the pretty path through the old neighborhood of tasteful houses.

This way has the added bonus of winding around so that they'll pass the Starbucks and can pick up coffee to have with their desserts. (Yes, they are still planning on eating dessert, no matter how full they feel.)

Ivy loves the tree-lined streets. They pass one beautiful house after another, a few with for sale signs out front, and even more that evoke a feeling that the inhabitants have been there for decades and have no plans to ever live anywhere else.

"I like this one," Jason says, pointing at a large home with a large inviting wrap-around porch.

"That's a good one," Ivy agrees. "I love the porch swing. My favorite house is up here on the right."

"Of course, you have a favorite," Jason says warmly.

"Always planning for my big lottery win!" Ivy replies.

She pauses a moment later in front of a Mediterranean home with a small balcony off what appears, from the glimpse through the oversized windows, to be a book-lined office. But it is not just the home itself that is so impressive, it's also the landscaping. The yard seems to have combined the meandering beauty of an English garden with the native plants of California making the house feel like it may be hidden in the middle of a forest while also clearly being meticulously well maintained.

"Ooh, that yard is amazing. Nice choice. Have you seen inside?" Jason asks as they continue to walk.

"Not in person, no. It sold a few years ago and I saw pictures from the listing. You can't see it with all the trees, but it has lots of shaded patios, balconies, and even a little guest house. It was bright and cheery inside and it has a good-sized lot so there would be room for me to build the run I want for Toby."

"The enclosed one that will keep him safe from wildlife, right?"

"Yes! Have I mentioned this before?" Ivy asks, a little embarrassed.

"Yes, but it was a while ago. And it's a very good idea," Jason replies, letting her know she has nothing to be embarrassed about. "So, basically, when you mention *your* dream home, you really mean that you need to win the lottery for Toby."

"Basically," Ivy replies with a nod.

"Are you ready to head back home? I can place our Starbucks order," Jason offers, reaching for his phone.

"No. I mean, yes, I'm ready to head back, but no to you buying Starbucks. You bought that amazing dinner. Let me treat you to a birthday latte, at least," Ivy says, pulling out her phone. She places their order, and they continue to admire the homes as they walk.

When they turn the corner, they see a few men coming their way, taking up the entire sidewalk and not wearing any masks. An unfortunately frequent occurrence in her neighborhood. Ivy looks over her shoulder to see if it's clear to step into the street to get around them, but Jason takes her hand, guiding her behind him as he proceeds to confidently walk on the sidewalk forcing the men to either walk single file or walk straight into him.

The men begrudgingly move over so they only take up only their half of the sidewalk.

The moment Jason takes hold of Ivy's hand, she pictures that classic shot of Darcy's hand in her favorite Pride and Prejudice. An oft alluded to moment among romantics, but not something that should make a woman of Ivy's age and experience get butterflies. She tries to curtail her silliness by reasoning that he's probably in the habit of holding hands from years and years of holding his wife's hand. It's just routine for him, surely.

"Your hand is freezing," Jason says.

"Poor circulation," Ivy replies and instead of dropping her hand, Jason takes her other one and just holds them between his own hands to warm them.

"Better?" he asks.

"Much. Thank you. I once dated a guy who would get annoyed when I tried to hold his hand because mine are always cold. I'd have to breathe on them or rub them together or something to warm them before I touched him."

"Sounds like a keeper," Jason says and Ivy laughs.

"I mean, I understand not wanting ice-cold fingers grabbing your dick, but just handholding?" Ivy says. "That's just being dramatic."

Jason laughs and releases one of her hands so they can walk more easily, but he still holds the other one, and continues to hold it until they reach Starbucks where he drops it only to open the door for them. They pick up their drinks and head back home, walking a block in amiable silence until Ivy breaks it, with what can only seem to Jason to be a random question, but which followed Ivy's train of thought since he grabbed her hand.

"Have you ever had a crush?" she asks.

"What?" Jason asks. "Of course, I have."

"It's not a crazy question. For me, a crush is someone you obsess over but that you don't actually ever get. And it seems like you got the woman you wanted, so it's not unreasonable to think you just never had a crush. A real-life crush, I mean. Not a celebrity."

"In elementary school, I was madly in love with Casey Bartlett. She was so cute, and she let me use her markers once in first grade, so I loved her from that day until probably fourth grade when her family moved."

"And was she the last one?" Ivy asks.

Jason hesitates a moment then says, "I probably had some other crushes before I started dating Nicole. I just can't think of any right now. Casey was memorable because she was my first." He looks at Ivy and asks her, "How about you?"

"Oh lord, there are too many to count. I used to develop crushes so easily. Well, honestly, maybe I still do. The slightest act of common decency a man shows and I'm in love. But I'm trying to learn from past mistakes and I will no longer accept the bare minimum from men," Ivy says proudly.

"Good, you deserve better than just common decency, or an ass who won't hold your icy Elsa hand," Jason says.

When they get back to their building, Jason runs up to his apartment to get the desserts and change into what he calls, "big belly bottoms" (his elastic-waste flannels), a term Ivy finds adorable. They reconvene at her place about ten minutes later, in comfy clothes and ready to eat some cake and watch some TV.

The two sit on Ivy's couch, forking their cake directly into their mouths from the plastic shells they were packed in rather than dirtying actual plates, Gilmore Girls cued up but on pause while they talk. Though still a little too full to be eating anything else, Ivy does a happy dance with each bite.

"Why is chocolate so damn good?" Ivy says, almost moaning as she savors the rich moist cake.

"I don't know, but this cheesecake is fucking amazing."

"Do you think we should postpone our GG marathon and watch one of the shows everyone keeps talking about?" Ivy asks. "Are we missing out on all the cool pandemic trends?"

"Like what? Tiger King?"

"That's one example. I can't imagine that it's good, but my friend did say I should watch it. But then if it's got animal abuse, I don't know how it can be fun," Ivy says.

"I'm not ready for anything new at the moment. My brain can't handle it. So, if you're okay with sticking with the Gilmores, that would be my choice."

"I am definitely okay with that," Ivy replies. "I enjoy watching TV with you, no matter what we watch," she continues, genuinely meaning it, but saying it in a playful way and topping it off with an exaggerated smile where she flashes him her teeth purposely covered in chocolate cake.

"Oh wow. That's so sweet," Jason says, dryly.

They each eat half their cakes, putting the rest back in the fridge, and sip their lattes as they watch the show. About halfway through the second episode, Ivy starts feeling restless and begins tapping Jason with her bootie-covered feet, which she has extended on the couch.

"I don't think my latte was decaf," Ivy says. "We might need to walk Toby. I don't know if I can sit still."

"Uh oh. Do you need to go run around the block? Will a Toby-paced walk be enough?" Jason asks, smiling as he watches Ivy practically vibrating with energy.

"I don't know!" she replies. "You want to wrestle?"

"No," Jason says, laughing. "I think you're going to kill me."

"Wuss!"

"My dear, you have crazy eyes right now. I don't feel safe letting you pin me down," he says.

"*Letting* me pin you? Why do you think I couldn't actually pin you?" Ivy asks.

"I don't think I mentioned this, but I wrestled in high school. I was pretty good," Jason replies.

"But did you ever wrestle above your weight class with someone who had crazy lady caffeine strength?"

"I did not. You've got me there. But I still think I can take you," he replies, teasingly.

"Fine! Let's take Toby out. But if he wants to sniff a lot, I might have to leave him with you and just run to the park and back."

Ivy jumps up from the couch and practically runs to the cabinet by the door to grab Toby's harness and leash, theatrically calling Toby's name in an operatic tone. After a moment, Toby sluggishly comes out of her room, having clearly been fast asleep. While she waits for him to slowly walk into the living room, she dances in place a bit.

"Do you want to put your shoes on while you wait?" Jason asks, thoroughly amused by what he's witnessing.

"Oh yah, that's a good idea," Ivy says and dramatically wraps Toby's leash, harness already attached, loosely around her neck like a scarf, then drops to the floor to put on her shoes.

"Honestly, I think I might give you caffeine every night," Jason says with a smile. "This is very entertaining."

"It's all fun and games until someone gets hurt!" she replies. "Or until I crash in a couple of hours."

After putting her shoes on, Ivy crawls over to Toby who has finally walked his sleepy ass most of the way to her. Once his harness dance is complete and she's got him hooked up, they all rush down the hallway, a little faster and a lot louder than usual. The moment they are outside, Toby stops to sniff and mark.

"Goddamn it! Get your shit together, Toby!" Ivy says, slightly startling a man who had the misfortune of coming around the corner at the same time.

"We've had a little too much caffeine," Jason says to the man, doing a friendly head nod that he hopes communicates something along the lines of, "Don't worry," or "Don't call PETA."

Ivy turns to Jason and hands him Toby's leash, "I need to run. You stay with him!" And as soon as Jason takes hold of the leash, Ivy is gone. Toby looks up in confusion, whining for a moment as he watches Ivy leave, but Jason is able to reassure him, and Toby goes back to sniffing.

A moment later, Jason and Toby make their way around the corner, Jason expecting to see Ivy's fleeing form already at the other end of the block, but instead, he sees something in the grass, not too far off and realizes it's her. He and Toby jog over to check on her.

"Are you okay?" Jason asks with concern, before realizing Ivy is laughing hysterically. "Oh my god. What the hell happened?"

"My knee gave out," Ivy squeaks out when she can catch her breath. "I forgot I can't run."

"You are probably lying in dog shit. Definitely in dog pee. You have to get up."

Pointing this out only makes Ivy laugh harder, which makes Toby rush to her face to lick her, which, in turn, makes her laugh even more. Smiling, Jason glances up and down the block to see if anyone is coming. Luckily, the coast is clear, so Ivy has time to pull herself together and get up, if only to get away from Toby licking her face.

"Okay," Ivy says as Jason helps her stand. "I think that did it. I think I'm good. I got my energy out."

Jason gives her a once-over. "Well, I don't see any obvious feces on you, so you chose a good place to collapse."

"I haven't run in a decade. My caffeine brain was writing checks my old body couldn't cash," Ivy says, still winded from her laughter.

They continue their walk, which is unusually fast paced since Toby is now hyped up from all the commotion, and they're all back to Ivy's much sooner than usual. Ivy is noticeably calmer now.

"Honestly, I think they put meth in my latte," she says.

"Or maybe an extra shot."

"It's definitely one or the other," Ivy says, her face still lit up from her laughing fit. "I am going to go change, just in case these clothes are now covered in animal waste or whatever."

"Good idea," Jason says. "Toby and I will wait here. A safe distance from any lingering caffeine urges."

But when Ivy returns in her pajamas and sees Jason, it seems she does still have some residual energy, just not so much that it's shooting straight out of her, but she's not ready to relax yet. "You wanna play a game or something?" she asks. "I have Twister!"

"Do you really?"

"No. I wish. That would be perfect. But I do have," and she lists as she counts them on her fingers, "Connect Four, Sorry, a very old version of Disney Trivia, and several decks of cards."

Jason selects Connect Four and Ivy unearths the game from her closet, claiming the black checkers as hers and giving Jason the red. They move to the kitchen table and before they begin playing, Ivy selects a station on her phone so they can listen to some music. So obviously, before long, Ivy is chair-dancing, which is quite similar to her hootenanny choreography.

"You're trying to distract me with your moves," Jason says. "But it won't work. I'm far too focused."

"Oh yah?" Ivy asks, eyebrow raised.

And she begins to do as sexy of a dance as someone sitting in their pajamas at a kitchen table playing an 80's game and listening to 90's pop music can do, a mix of a sort of a hair tousle and a boob thrust which stops immediately when it's her turn to go. She considers returning to her teasingly sexy moves as soon as she drops her piece into the yellow grid, but the look on Jason's face is not the one of encouraging amusement she expected, so she doesn't continue.

Despite all his concentration, Ivy beats him, and Jason is forced to watch a brief victory dance that makes him smile. After she wins four out of five games, she begins to feel the caffeine crash set in, but not wanting Jason to leave yet, she considers proposing another game. Jason has other plans.

"It's getting late. I'll try beating you at Disney Trivia another time," Jason says teasingly.

"Oh, dear sir, if you think I was good at Connect Four, I am amazing at late 90's edition Disney Trivia," she says, her confidence betrayed a bit by a badly suppressed yawn. "I will crush you."

"You won't be able to stay awake long enough to crush me."

"Sounds like you're chicken," Ivy says with a goading smirk.

"Are you trying to bait me?" Jason asks, eyebrow raised.

"I sure am."

"Look, you don't know this about me, but my parents took us to Disneyland when I was five years old, and I was obsessed with everything Disney for the next decade until I learned that it wasn't cool for teenaged boys to like kid's cartoons. So, prepare to lose."

"Baited!"

"And I raise you a challenge," he says with a mischievous look in his eye.

"Oh?"

"Strip Disney Trivia!"

"Done!" Ivy replies. "And by the way, the fact that I didn't even hesitate to let someone see me naked in a well-lit kitchen should scare the shit out of you. That's how badly I'm going to crush you."

Ivy pulls the game out of the closet and makes a point of wiping off the dust from the gold, round tin in front of Jason, who laughs at her theatrics.

"I get it, you haven't recently memorized all the cards," Jason says.

"I just don't want to hear you making excuses later, after you've lost. And you're sad. And emasculated."

"Is it emasculating to lose at Disney Trivia?"

"I wouldn't know, I've never lost." Ivy replies haughtily.

Jason cannot even reply to that, he just chuckles and shakes his head at this new tough, competitive persona Ivy has adopted. They set up the game, which is essentially Trivial Pursuit but with Disney categories and everything that can be in the shape of Mickey's head is in the shape of Mickey's head. They roll to see who goes first, and Ivy, once again, wins.

"Wait. Let's be clear on the rules. Are we taking off clothes when we get one wrong, or when the other person gets one right?" Jason asks.

"Great question. I'll let you decide. How fast do you want to be naked?"

He lets that dig slide and says, "I say anytime the other person gets any question right. *And* anytime you get one wrong. First person naked loses."

"Oh my god, you're going to be nude in a matter of seconds," Ivy says with a sneer. She rolls to start the game and lands on the category of Animation, Jason reads the question.

"In the Disney cartoon about Lambert the lion, what kind of animal does Lambert think he is?" As soon as Jason is done reading the question, he checks the back of the card for the answer and looks Ivy in the eyes, giving her his own smirk, sure that she will not know the answer since he didn't.

"Oh, do you mean Lambert, the sheepish lion? Lambert who is always trying to be a wild and wooly sheep? Lambert, the sheepish lion?" she says, not quite singing the answer, but making it clear that it is definitely a song.

And it is at that moment that Jason realizes he may have overplayed his hand a bit. "Lambert is a lion who thinks he's a sheep," Ivy concludes.

"Correct."

Ivy makes a victory gesture with her fist and then smiles at Jason, expectantly. He removes his sock and Ivy does a polite golf clap.

Approximately ten minutes later, Jason sits at the table in just his flannel pants and, presumably, his underwear. Ivy has gotten her first question wrong, so she removes one sock.

"Look," Ivy says, "I'm not a bully. I will let you change the rules for when you take clothes off now if you'd like."

"No, that's fine. My reign of terror is about to begin. Get ready to get naked," Jason replies. He answers a question about DuckTales correctly, so Ivy removes her other sock and then her hoodie after he is able to answer another pretty mainstream question, but his promised reign of terror ends quickly. At Ivy's second turn, he's already down to just his underwear.

"I think I've made my point. We can stop here," Ivy says in a conciliatory manner. "You don't have to get naked. But! You do have to admit that I kicked your ass and that you know nothing about Disney and I know everything."

"I will admit that you kicked my ass," Jason says, but then he continues in a playfully antagonistic tone. "But I think you just got lucky."

"Wow. The male ego is a fascinating creature," Ivy replies. "You would rather sit there, completely naked, your bare ass and balls sliming up my chair than just admit that I have superior knowledge? About Disney? Really?"

"Look, one tricky question and it's back to me. I can still win this," Jason says. "But more importantly, my ass and balls aren't slimy!"

"We're going to see, because you're about to be naked!" Ivy declares.

Jason's gamble pays off as Ivy cannot answer a question about some straight to video sequel and she is forced to choose between her T-shirt and her pants. Remembering she is wearing a flattering bra, she opts to remove her shirt, maybe even hoping to distract him some. She is pleased to see that Jason is having trouble taking his eyes off her chest and even more pleased that her stomach is mostly hidden by the table. She made the right choice.

Unfortunately for Jason, his question is also about a straight to video sequel only a small child would have watched, so with that wrong question, it's time to pay up. Ivy sets her elbows on the table, links her fingers together, and places her chin on her hands. Then she smiles at him and makes a point of batting her eyelashes, obviously preparing to see the goods. "Let's see it."

Jason takes in her gloating grin and smiles back. "I think things got a little out of hand, don't you?" he says with an endearing smile, totally backpedaling.

"Nope! You were given a few opportunities to prevent this. You decided not to. I'm not going to *force* you to keep your end of the bargain, but ..." She raises her eyebrows as she trails off.

"Is this really what you want?" Jason asks.

"Doesn't matter. I *earned* it," Ivy says with a smug grin. "Or, you need to admit that I am not only better than you at Connect Four and Disney Trivia, but in general. In all things. Completely and totally superior."

Jason hesitates a moment but is not yet ready to concede to her game night superiority. Standing, he puts his hands to the waistband of his boxer briefs. He is fully intending to remove them, just to see her reaction because he's pretty sure she doesn't think he'll actually do it. He wants to call her bluff.

But then he looks at her smiling face and at her there in front of him in her bra and a rush of genuine longing comes over him and, all of a sudden, this feels more like foreplay than a fun game between friends. He releases his waistband and puts a hand out for Ivy to shake and says, "You are the superior person in all regards."

Ivy notices the change in his demeanor, so she doesn't goad him further. She's not quite sure what shifted, but she stands and takes his hand

and gives a sportsman-like shake. And then there is a very real, very awkward moment where they are just standing in front of each other, in their underwear.

Trying to break the weirdness, Ivy says, "We should probably get dressed. Now that I kicked your ass." But the playful mood from before is gone and what's left is just good old-fashioned sexual tension. There is an obvious pause when both should be reaching for their clothes to get dressed, but they're not.

"I really want to kiss you," Jason says, his voice suddenly slightly raspy.

"I really want you to kiss me," Ivy replies.

Jason takes a step closer and continues, "But we discussed how that's a bad idea."

"We did. And it probably is," Ivy replies, as she also steps closer to him. "I just can't remember why right now."

And then Jason's hands are on Ivy's face, pulling her into him and her hands are on his solid chest, moving around to his back. This is not their first kiss, but something is most definitely different this time. As Ivy becomes fully aware of their bodies pressing against each other, she has that familiar feeling she's gotten with Jason, a feeling of doing something she's done before but it feeling completely new with him. She has no idea how long they stay in the kitchen, just exploring each other, like they can't get enough of just touching and kissing.

Ivy's hands haven't even gone below his waist, perfectly content to soak in the feeling of his chest, back and arms. From months of purposely keeping apart, their guards are down and now they're making up for lost time.

When they eventually move into the bedroom and their remaining clothes are tossed to the floor, Ivy is genuinely content. This is what she has been looking for, a real emotional connection with someone who cares about her *and* a physical connection. As their bodies move together in pleasure, she has a very clear thought of, "Oh! *This* is what it's supposed to be."

Later, as they lie in bed together, cuddling in a very satisfied afterglow and chatting in the easy way they always do, it feels very comfortable and just *right*. They fall asleep, Ivy still in Jason's arms, and she honestly isn't sure she's ever been so happy.

Ivy awakens a few hours later by movement in the bedroom. She opens her eyes slightly to see Jason grabbing his clothes. She waits silently for a second to give him a chance to say something to her. Or at least kiss her on the forehead before he goes. Instead, Ivy watches silently as he leaves.

CHAPTER 27

The next morning, Ivy checks her phone. Nothing from Jason. It's still a little early for him, so she lets that slide and takes Toby out for his morning walk, feeds him, and sits down to debate what to do next.

She could just text Jason. It's not uncommon for her to text him first, she's usually up several hours before he is. Of course, she's not the one who snuck out in the middle of the night, so it sort of seems like the chicken-shit who did that should be the one to make the first move today. But she'll be the mature one.

> IVY
> Where the fuck did you go??!?!?!??!!?

No, probably not. Ivy thinks as she erases that. *It would be hard to read that with humor right now.* Ivy tries again. *Nothing accusatory. Aim for casual curiosity.*

> IVY
> Good morning. Where'd you go? Was I
> snoring?

Not bad, it's relatively friendly, casual, and it doesn't immediately accuse him of being an asshole. She hits send and then puts her phone down and goes into the kitchen to make breakfast, doing her best to ignore her phone completely.

Ivy soon realizes that not listening to anything to distract her just lets her overthink what happened, so she puts in her earbuds and silences her phone. That way, even if Jason does reply, she won't know right away and won't look too needy. Ivy selects Whitney Houston's "It's Not Right, But It's Okay" on her phone and really does her best to think about literally anything other than Jason.

After listening to several similar selections from Spotify and finishing her breakfast, which she consumed almost unconsciously, there is still no text from Jason. But she tells herself that it's still relatively early for someone who left her apartment at 3AM, so there's no need to worry, yet.

But even after she takes Toby for a very long walk, comes home, showers, and does her full hair and makeup, she hasn't received anything from him. In fact, he does not respond until the late afternoon.

JASON
No, nothing you did. We should probably talk
though. Dinner tonight?

Ivy is relieved that he finally texted her back, but his response does not offer the comfort she was hoping for and she feels like she might vomit. A feeling of impending doom engulfs her and she very intentionally does not respond so that she doesn't type anything she regrets. Putting her phone down, she takes a few deep breaths and thinks about what to say.

Unfortunately, her attempt to be reasonable and not lash out is not working. The adrenaline and panic are setting in, so she focuses on her breathing. She has been ghosted before, spending a day or two wondering if there was a problem and making excuses only to face the fact that she's never going to hear from that guy again. And she has been dumped plenty. Ivy is no stranger to the dread of meeting up with someone or calling someone absolutely knowing it was going to be terrible and awkward. But the fact that *Jason* might pull that shit with her is too much.

In a moment of clarity, or maybe rage, she decides she is not going to put herself through the torment of waiting several hours just to endure a difficult talk about what a mistake they made. She grabs her essentials: keys, phone, and mask. She gives Toby a brisk, "I'll be right back," on her way out the door.

She knocks on Jason's door more aggressively than she had planned. But to be honest, she doesn't have full control of her limbs right now. After a moment, she hears him unlocking the door and when he opens it, she says with what she meant to be a cheery tone, but came out as a sort of manic voice, "Hey, can I come in?"

Ivy pushes by him, not waiting for him to answer. She's torn for a second between taking the time to remove her shoes so she can move beyond Jason's established quarantine zone and maybe sit down like two mature adults and just staying where she is, by the door, so she can make a quick retreat, if needed.

"I don't think 'we need to talk' has ever been followed by a good conversation. So, I'd rather get this over with and not spend the rest of the day dreading your visit. What did you want to say to me?" Ivy asks.

"I hadn't decided yet."

A completely humorless laugh escapes before Ivy can stop it. "Great. Well, let me start. Why did you sneak out of my apartment in the middle of the night?" stopping herself from adding, "Like a little bitch."

"Because I'm a piece of shit," Jason offers, no humor in his tone.

This admission only makes her angrier. "So, why did you do it?"

"I know what it looks like to you, but I don't regret sleeping with you," Jason says.

Ivy gives him plenty of time to continue, but he doesn't and with each disappointment in him, each dagger to the heart, she regrets allowing herself to be this hurt. She wasn't supposed to be falling for him. And this right here is why. As his silence fills the room, she decides to respond. "Thank you, I guess? 'I don't regret sleeping with you' is just what every girl wants to hear."

"I'm afraid I ruined what we had," Jason says.

"Do you mean because we had sex or because you ran away after?" He doesn't answer and Ivy continues, seething. "I'm a good *friend*, right?"

Emphatically he tries. "Yes, your friendship is important to m-"

Ivy doesn't want to hear it. "I get it. You're not attracted to me, except for the times when you, what? Lower your standards? When you've been alone too long? Like in a moment of weakness or something? Is that it?"

"I *am* attracted to you," he replies.

"Us having sex didn't have to ruin anything. You treating me like someone you're embarrassed to have had sex with is the problem."

"I just panicked."

"What made you panic?"

"I don't," Jason stammers, "I don't know. I'm really sorry. I know I'm not making sense."

"To me, panic pretty clearly signals regret."

"No, that's not it. Not like you're thinking."

"Let me be clear. I've been a consolation prize before, but I never would have expected *you* to treat me like that."

"That's not how I think of you at all. Please-" Jason steps forward to take Ivy's hand, but she tugs it back from his grip, almost backing into the door in an attempt to get away from him. He moves away giving her plenty of space. "I told you, I'm not myself right now. I'm broken. I don't know what I want. I know I like you. I know you're a wonderful person, and I just- I'm happy when I'm with you."

"Yah, you're so happy, you escaped in the middle of the night! I watched you leave! You didn't even glance at me!" Ivy says, her eyes beginning to fill with tears.

When Jason sees that, he can't help but start to tear up himself because he knows these are well-earned tears that *he* caused. "I really wish I hadn't done that. I want to be with you, but I'm not ready yet."

Hearing that triggers something in Ivy. She has a familiar feeling of being less than, like she's a good standby for the future, if all else fails. "Well, here's something you didn't even think about. Maybe *I* don't want to be with *you*. That never even occurred to you, did it? I must just be madly in love with you, right? It's just assumed that pathetic, fat Ivy must be in love with handsome you. You're freaking out about a commitment, and it never even occurred to you to ask if I wanted to be committed to *you*."

Jason takes a moment to formulate his response, knowing he doesn't have many more chances to get things right. "I didn't ask you how you felt because I assumed we were on the same page. I assumed you felt the same about me as I feel about you."

"Okay, so tell me how you feel about me," Ivy says, daring him to bare his soul.

His words come more freely now. "I think you're a warm, caring, funny person. I feel lucky to have met you. I'm home when I'm with you. And you must know that I find you attractive, I haven't hidden that. I feel like the person I was or the person I might become could make you happy. And we could be happy together. But this person," and Jason gestures up and down, indicating the man standing before her, "is not good enough for you."

Ivy does not immediately know what to do with that information. Her first inclination is to just hold him and assure him that they should be together, that they can work things out together. That she can help him. Then she remembers all the times she's tried to make broken relationships work, how many times she's been hurt. How many times she's waited and waited for someone who didn't chose her and instead of reaching for him, she says, "Well, you're right then. We are on the same page."

Jason looks up at her and she can see that he has a second of hope that he maybe said the right thing, but Ivy continues, "You're not good enough for me."

And Jason watches silently as she leaves

CHAPTER 28

Ivy takes Toby on an extra-long walk before bed, making sure she is not home if Jason decides to try to talk. She slips back into the building and into her apartment as quickly as possible, half-assedly washes her face, skips most of her nighttime routine and gets into her most comfortable pajamas before climbing into bed to let herself cry.

But now that she is allowing herself to let it all out, she has nothing. She's more numb than upset right now.

The next day, Ivy is simultaneously relieved and pissed that Jason hasn't texted her. She decides to keep to her schedule, theorizing that it's more likely she'll run into him if *she* changes anything. Her walks seem lonely, her time at home strangely empty. How did she let herself get so attached to a man who made it clear he did not want a relationship? Why does she always do this?

Having gone through the motions of the day for nearly a whole week, Ivy calls Holly for their Friday night chat. She considers telling Holly she is sick and needs to skip this week's episode and catch-up, but she decides it would be nice to speak to someone she knows loves her.

"Hello!" Holly says in a goofy British accent. And Ivy begins to sob.

"I'm okay," Ivy manages to say between gasping breaths.

"Is Toby okay?" Holly asks, concerned.

"Yes. We're both fine. Everyone's fine."

"That's good," Holly says, giving Ivy some time to get to a speaking point, she continues. "Then I'm just going to take a wild guess and say this has something to do with the man you're trying to pretend you don't love."

"Good guess. Fuck you." Ivy says, a slight laugh coming through her sobs.

And she explains what happened, telling Holly how Jason left, how they fought, how they left things, and how he has not tried to talk to her since.

"Look, I don't know this guy," Holly says, "But it sounds like he's going through some shit. Maybe he just needs some time to think things through."

"Maybe. But I'm just sick of being the girl who lets herself be treated badly by men. I'm trying to finally fucking learn from my mistakes! I would rather be alone than in another shitty relationship. But then I also feel like a bitch, like I could have been more understanding."

"You've got a lot of feelings going on there," Holly says, in a supportive but gently teasing tone.

"Here's the thing, I'm sick of putting in all the work. This is not someone I've been in a long-term relationship with who's going through a rough patch. If he were, I would definitely be there for him, I would support him. This is someone I don't have a long history with and who is currently not treating me how I want to be treated and who I don't know will ever be the person he wants to be or be someone who is ever going to be able to commit!" Ivy takes a breath, pointedly ending her frustrated rant.

"If that's how you feel, then you made the right choice," Holly responds. "But that doesn't mean you're not going to still have some amount of regret or feel bad about it." Ivy just sniffs into the phone as she thinks this over. "I think the best way to move on from this is avoidance. And psychologist will tell you that, I'm sure. Run away and come visit me. You finally have a nice new car that can make the journey, pack up Toby and get your ass out here."

CHAPTER 29

Jason spends Monday morning in a series of soul-sucking meetings and when he's finally done, he decides to take a walk. His destination? Literally anywhere but his fucking apartment. He has frenetic energy he needs to release.

As he walks toward the park, debating whether he should walk somewhere for lunch or maybe for coffee or just see how far he can walk before he snaps out of the funk he's in, he sees Otto waving to him from the other side of the street a few buildings down. Jason waves back and reluctantly crosses the street. He's not in the mood to talk to anyone but doesn't want to be rude.

"Hey! I haven't seen you in a while," Otto says, his usual cheerful voice booming from a considerable distance.

Jason waits to reply until they're closer, unable to match Otto's enthusiasm or volume. "Yah, I've sort of been busy with work," Jason says, which is a lie, but Otto doesn't need to hear that he has been depressed and hiding in his apartment.

"Where's Ivy? When I do see you outside lately, it's usually with her."

"Oh, yah. Just me, sorry."

Otto's uncanny knack of going from friendly to meddling kicks in, "Oh, that's okay. It's just nice to see you together. You're both such nice people, it's nice when nice people find each other."

"Yes, that is nice," Jason echoes. He considers correcting Otto to make it clear that they weren't dating, but a world where he and Ivy are together and just temporarily apart sounds nice. And Jason takes a moment to enjoy that fantasy. The pause this creates is long enough that correcting Otto after that would be weird.

"Plus, Toby's videos are very popular, so I always like getting good footage of him," Otto continues, never allowing a moment of silence.

Jason engages in polite chitchat for as long as he can before he excuses himself to walk home. His determination to get out of his apartment has been switched to a strong desire to get the hell away from all people.

"I'd better head back, I've got a meeting coming up," Jason says, already starting to walk toward the park exit."

"Okay, have a good day. Tell Ivy I said 'hi'," Otto replies.

Jason just nods in reply.

As he walks back home, he can't help but obsess over Ivy. Again. Jason thinks about Ivy a lot. Nearly constantly, in fact. He was really hoping a walk would clear his head, but even if he hadn't run into Otto, it probably wouldn't have worked.

His thoughts are cyclical, usually triggered by seeing something he wants to share with Ivy and then realizing he can't. But just the thought of her makes him remember the happy memories he has of their walks, their evenings hanging out, and of course *that* night. Then it's only a matter of time for those good thoughts to lead him directly to the ones where he remembers how much he fucked up.

He remembers waking up next to Ivy in bed *that* night and looking over at her. He wanted to hold her. He wanted to spend the rest of his fucking life holding her. It was a moment of absolute certainty, the emotional equivalent of "Oh, that's my forever person," and then that joy was immediately replaced by panic when he thought of how much he loved Nicole and how sure he was they would always be together.

He cringes thinking about how he got up, grabbed his clothes, and just left. Remembering it now, he actually has to shake his head to try to physically clear his mind of the thought.

As soon as Jason is back in his apartment, he pulls out his phone and makes a call. He's slightly relieved when he gets her voicemail and can leave a brief message. "Hi, Nicole. It's Jason. Um, I was hoping we could talk. Please call or text me."

CHAPTER 30

Though Holly wants Ivy to visit right away, Ivy needs time to properly prepare for a solo road trip. She's too much of an anxious traveler to just pack up and head out.

Her planning begins online as she prices emergency road-side kits, Googles what to do if her car breaks down in an area without a phone signal, watches videos on how to change a tire, and has Toby's expensive prescription diet auto-shipped directly to her sister's house so she doesn't have to pack it in her car.

Ivy also has to figure out what to bring so she can work from her sister's house for as long as possible. After all of those small details are sorted, she books her hotel in Utah and plans her route to Denver, along with which towns she should stop in for gas and bathroom breaks.

Next, Ivy starts her packing list, which is an almost pointless task because she will, inevitably, forget to pack something anyway. It's just the way she is. But it helps her anxiety to make a list so when she thinks of something, she can just add it to the list and then forget about it.

Ivy usually puts up her Christmas tree on Black Friday and since she'll be out of town at that time, she comes up with the wonderful plan to decorate for Christmas before leaving for Colorado. That way, she can come home to a magical Christmas wonderland.

So, at the time of the year she would usually be debating whether or not she wanted to bother with Halloween decorations, at home or at work, she's Christmas shopping!

She buys what any normal human would dub an 'excessive amount' of white twinkle lights, hangs garlands on anything that can hold one, sets up her Christmas tree leaving no ornament unhung, and buys a few mini cinnamon brooms from Trader Joe's. Her place is a cozy winter wonderland a full two months before Christmas.

Ivy plans on stopping in Vegas for gas, then on to her hotel in Utah. It's going to be a long drive, but she has snacks for both her and Toby, water, and an extensive playlist ready on her phone.

This is Toby's first road trip and after about thirty minutes of suspicious stares at Ivy, he eventually realizes they aren't headed to the vet and relaxes in his car bed.

About one day, one disgusting public restroom, a secluded hotel, and a lot of winding mountain roads later, Ivy parks in the alley behind Holly's house. Toby is excited and anxious when Ivy puts it into park, his trigger that whatever journey they are on is at an end. He puts his front paws on the middle console, like he always does when he wants to see where they are. Toby begins to cry slightly when he doesn't recognize anything.

But a moment later, Holly comes out to greet them and Toby begins to excitedly wag his tail at her, now crying from excitement. Holly has only visited them in LA a few times, but Toby loved her the moment they met.

Ivy busies herself making a few trips to bring in all the stuff from her car as Holly watches Toby explore her yard, then inside her house. As soon as Ivy is done settling in, she sits down on Holly's fluffy couch and takes a moment to relax, Toby jumping up next to her and putting his front paws on her leg, excitedly panting. She pets him and he makes himself comfortable next to her on the couch.

"Well, Toby approves. We can stay!" Ivy declares.

"Oh good. I'm glad my house is acceptable to a neurotic terrier," Holly replies.

"Toby has the highest of standards, so it's really quite a compliment."

After a quick recap of her journey for Holly, Ivy changes into her pajamas and grabs a couple of blankets from the pile in the hall closet.

"Has your house always been this cold? I'm freezing!" Ivy says, settling on the couch as Holly sits, blanket-free in her oversized chair.

"Yes, you freeze every time you visit," Holly replies. "Because you've become an LA wuss."

With a few hours before dinner, Ivy shares her remaining car snacks with Holly and they turn on Deadpool, their traditional go-to movie and Ivy makes it through about fifteen minutes before she is fast asleep. Holly only manages to stay up for about ten minutes beyond that.

They both wake up when the end credits begin to play, both ready to eat a real meal. They decide on tacos and as Holly starts pulling out the necessary ingredients, Ivy stands out of the way, helping only when told to, as is tradition.

After dinner, Ivy does the dishes and decides to call it a night, though it is still another hour and a half before she is actually in bed, she and Holly having begun to chat while doing their nightly routines.

They awake next morning with about nine inches of snow so Ivy pulls out the sweater she bought for Toby before they left and slides it on him. She and Holly watch from the back door as Toby, who has only ever lived in Los Angeles, investigates this new substance.

It immediately becomes clear that Toby is not a fan. The moment he steps off the porch and falls into the snow, which reaches his chest, he's done. He shoots Ivy a look that clearly says, "Bitch, what was that?" as he runs back inside.

CHAPTER 31

Jason sees Nicole seated at a picnic table in the shade of a large California oak and waves. As he walks over to her, he fights a sinking feeling that this was a terrible idea. But, it's too late now. He just has to make the best of it.

"Hi," Nicole says while debating whether she should get up and hug him or stay seated at the table.

Seeing her awkwardness lessens his own stress a bit. "You don't have to get up," Jason says as he sits down across from her.

"It's nice to see you. Well, to see most of you," she says, gesturing to the mask on her own face.

"Yah, nice to sort of see you too. Thank you for agreeing to meet with me. I know you must be really busy with the baby."

"I have been, which actually makes this a kind of nice break. You probably won't believe me, but I've missed you," Nicole replies. "And your mom has been worried about you, especially since Harry died."

Jason nods his head, but can't bring himself to comment on that, so Nicole continues, hesitantly.

"I wish you had let me say goodbye to him. I've missed him too. I've even missed occasionally stepping in pee when he couldn't quite make it onto the pad."

"Harry's death was sudden. Well, I mean, you know he was old, but I didn't plan on putting him down. He was still chugging along, but he had a seizure," Jason says the words still hard for him to say.

"I'm so sorry. Your mom didn't mention that. But I should have known you wouldn't . . . I know you're still mad at me and, obviously, you have good reason to be. But I should have known you wouldn't use Harry as a way to punish me."

There is a pause that is so full of things both of them want to say that it's almost as if there is no silence at all. But eventually, Jason speaks.

"Let me start by saying I am not proud of how I behaved during our divorce. I was hurt and angry and I wanted to punish you. But I just ended up punishing both of us. I wish I could have a do-over, but the best I can do is apologize now."

Even wearing her mask, Nicole's relief is obvious. "I completely understand that you were hurt. And you had every reason to be. I'm sure I would have been twice as horrible if the roles were reversed."

"Oh, four times as horrible at least," Jason says, extending his teasing as a peace offering.

"Ten times, is that better?" Nicole teases back. "I think I actually appreciated you making me feel bad. I knew I deserved it. It kept me from punishing myself. So, thank you?"

"You're welcome?" Jason replies, matching Nicole's unsure tone. "If it helps, I'll probably always be hurt and angry."

"Oddly enough, that doesn't actually help me. And if it's true, I doubt it's helping you either. But you're entitled to your feelings," Nicole replies.

"It's a little true. But forget about that. I wanted to talk to you about," Jason hesitates a moment before he spits the words out in a rush, "About what happened to our marriage."

"Well, this is going to be a delicate topic, but I'm impressed you want to discuss it."

"What did I do wrong?" Jason asks.

"Do you really think there's just one thing that you did?" Nicole shakes her head as if erasing what she just said. "I didn't mean it that way. I mean, do you think *you* are the only one to blame and it was just *one* mistake that ended our marriage? You have to know it's not that simple."

"Okay, then explain it to me. Because from my perspective, we had a good marriage. Things were going fine, then I learn you're not happy and you're sleeping with someone else." Jason does his best to remain calm and leave any anger out of his tone as he continues. "And then, before we can really even address anything or work on anything or try to fix anything, you're gone. If you're willing to throw away two decades of us for another man, how am I supposed to see things? How am I supposed to not see *me* as the issue?"

"If someone had told me five years ago that you and I wouldn't be together anymore, I wouldn't have believed them. You're a part of me, we grew up together! We became ourselves with each other."

"I agree."

"I can't explain how I got to a place where that wasn't enough for me anymore. I wish I had a clear-cut answer for you. But I don't. I think I started thinking of you more as a friend, maybe even a brother, and I didn't really even notice until someone else came along who felt more like a lover."

At her use of "lover" Jason thinks of Ivy and how much she would have hated that word. How she never would have said that. Or if she did, how she would have made a gagging noise after or made fun of herself.

It occurs to Jason that what Nicole just said should have hurt. It should have been salt to his wounds, but instead, he was thinking about Ivy. He wants her to be here, talking to Nicole, with him. Such a wholly inappropriate time for her to be with him, but it doesn't matter. He wants her here. He always wants her with him.

Which brings him back to this meeting. He came here today to figure out how to make things work with Ivy, to make sure his lingering hang-ups from his marriage don't ruin his future.

"So, was I not affectionate enough? Was that the issue?" Jason asks.

"I think we both got lazy about keeping things romantic between us. I think we'd been together so long, we just had our marriage on autopilot," Nicole says.

Jason doesn't reply and Nicole can't help but notice that he seems to be processing everything. Then something occurs to her.

"You've met someone," she states.

"What?" Jason asks, her words pulling him out of his head.

"You wanted to find out what went wrong with our marriage because you've met someone."

Jason hesitates a moment, then confesses. "Yes. I've met someone. And I need to figure out what's wrong with me so I don't fuck things up again if I manage to work things out with her."

Nicole laughs, more to herself than genuinely finding this funny. "Hey, if I have to struggle through making a new relationship work, so do you. No freebies from me."

Jason looks up at her. He sees the corners of her eyes crinkling and knows she's smiling at him. He misses her smile. Misses her face. But for the first time in a long time, thinking about her is more of a nostalgic twinge, like remembering a good time, not the stab to his heart it has been for so long.

"Do you mind if we take our masks off?" he asks. "I want to see your dumb old face."

Nicole laughs, "Yah, I want to see your dumb old face too."

Maskless, they take a moment just to look at one another. They each observe how the other's face, so familiar for so long, has changed in the time they've been apart. Maybe an extra wrinkle, maybe some gray in Jason's beard, but a feeling of ease falls over them both.

"I really wish I could point to one thing that either one of us could have fixed or could avoid in the future, but I can't." Nicole says. "And I'm sure that's as unhelpful and frustrating for you as it is for me. I'm constantly worried the happiness and contentment I feel in my marriage will just disappear one day. I'll just wake up and I won't feel it anymore."

"And I'm worried the happiness and contentment Ivy and I might have will disappear when *she* wakes up and doesn't feel it anymore."

"And that might happen. To either of us. But you can't avoid relationships because you're afraid you're going to end up with some cheating whore like me again," Nicole says, giving him her familiar joking smirk.

"I think you're more of a slut than a whore," he replies with a similar grin.

"Does this new girl love your pedantry?"

"Oh, I think all women do."

"So, are you going to tell me about her?"

And Nicole listens as Jason recounts how he and Ivy met and all the reasons he fell for her and how he hopes to show her how much he cares and convince her to give him a second chance. Nicole then shares how motherhood is going and how hard it's been but also how amazing. What it's like to now have a second daughter. And they're just two old friends catching up on a beautiful day in the park.

CHAPTER 32

It doesn't take long for Holly and Ivy to settle into a quaroutine that nicely mixes their work responsibilities with their traditional hanging-out pastimes. With the advantage of the yard, Ivy only has to walk Toby twice a day and many of the walks are cut short due to the biting cold.

The post-work walk usually also includes calling Anthony to check in and chat for a bit, but as soon as Toby and Ivy arrive back at Holly's, it's sister bonding time.

Holly and Ivy tend to watch the same movies and shows over and over and over, taking a break to make dinners that Ivy would never have the patience or skills to make on her own. Then after dinner, they'll play on their phones while a selection from their limited library plays in the background. Then dessert. Then bed.

Just to shake things up a bit, Holly suggests a new show from her watchlist. Ivy isn't much of a fantasy fan, but she agrees to watch The Witcher when Holly suggests it.

And thank God Ivy did because she hadn't actually seen Henry Cavill in anything before and she had no idea what she was missing. From this day forward, Ivy will consider her life being divided between After Henry (AH) and the dark times before this glorious day as BH.

Despite her enjoyment, several episodes in, it becomes obvious that Ivy has no idea what's going on.

"Wait, I thought we were out of the flash-back now. Isn't that lady dead?" Ivy asks.

"She's alive in this timeline," Holly replies.

"Wait, what? Is there more than one timeline? I thought there was just an occasional flashback."

"Have you even been paying attention to anything other than Henry?" Holly asks with a laugh.

"No. I guess not."

"There have been at least two continuous timelines so far," Holly explains, shaking her head.

"So, Geralt doesn't age?" Ivy exclaims.

"I don't think witchers or mages age like normal humans. If at all."

"And what's a mage again?" Ivy asks, mostly joking.

"Yennefer is a mage. All the people who perform magic are mages. But since Henry isn't one, I assume you didn't really notice them."

"Okay, but if a bunch of the main characters don't age, how was I supposed to know what was happening? Make it clear to me, I'm dumb. Cut Geralt's hair or something! Or better yet, have him topless in one timeline and sleeveless in another."

"Just naked in the third, if there is a third."

"Yes! I would definitely notice *that*. And then I'd have a new favorite show!"

"A new obsession and no social life. And probably lose your job. And soon Toby would be taught to pee on pads indoors so you could just stay on your couch 24/7 watching Henry sword fight," Holly jokes.

"I like this future you've created for me," Ivy smiles back. Then her attention is brought back to her phone when she hears it ding with Jason's text notification.

JASON
Hi. You have a lot of mail piling up in the lobby,
hope you're ok and just out of town. Let me
know if you want me to grab your mail for you.

Ivy briefly considers not responding and just letting Jason's imagination run wild with thoughts of her dead in her apartment like the lady in Apartment One as he debates how long he'll wait before he goes to the apartment to check on her. She could just call Mike, the useless building manager, and to ask him to collect her mail. And Jason can suck it.

But Mike would probably lose her mail or hoard it or something. And she doesn't *actually* want Jason to worry about her.

> IVY
> I'm fine. I'm in Colorado. I submitted a mail hold request, I guess the mail carrier ignored that

Jason replies so quickly he must have still been holding his phone.

Lock on Lockdown

JASON
Very glad you're ok
Do you want me to collect your mail?
I can even empty your mailbox, if you want
So there's not a chance of your mail just
sitting out
I still have your apartment key and I assume
your mailbox key is in the usual spot in the
drawer above where you keep Toby's leash
I can check your mail periodically until you get
back and just leave all of it in your place so
you don't have to see me when you return
Or outside your door
Whatever works for you
I'm going to stop typing now and let you
respond

Ivy smiles at the acknowledgement of his texting avalanche. She thinks over his offer, while also pettily taking her sweet time to reply. It's important to make it clear she has not, in any way, forgiven him. No quick, needy responses from her! But it would be silly to refuse his offer. I mean, he owes her, right? He broke her heart so it seems like he can, at the very least, gather her mail for her. That's fair.

> IVY
> Thank you. That would be helpful

JASON
...
...
How long will you be gone?

> IVY
> I don't know for sure. I was originally
> planning on just being here for
> Thanksgiving but I think I'll be able to
> stay away from work an extra week
> But if you aren't able to check my mail
> that long, I can call Mike

JASON
No, I'm not going anywhere
And Mike would probably just lose your mail
Or hoard it

Ivy smiles, again, when she reads that he had the same suspicion of Mike that she had. Unfortunately, it's at the same time Holly looks over at her.

"Uh oh. What cute thing did Jason say?" Holly asks.

"Nothing cute," Ivy replies, not even needing to ask how she knew it was Jason. She types out a quick thank you to Jason without mentioning their shared thought, silences her phone, and leaves it on the table, returning her attention to the TV.

Jason waits a moment to see if she'll type anything else. He was really hoping Ivy would continue to text with him a little longer, but after replying to her thank you text, there's nothing more from her. He grabs the mail he already collected for her from his table then goes down to her place to get the mailbox key.

When he lets himself in, he is greeted by the scent of cinnamon and a whole lot of Christmas décor. He pauses for a moment, taking in the tree, the lights strung up everywhere, garlands, bobbles, and what appears to be a few dozen boxes worth of candy canes hung everywhere. He smiles imagining Ivy's excitement in doing all of these and describing this over-the-top design as "Christmas threw up". He thinks about turning on all the lights and just hanging out there for the rest of the night.

After emptying out her mailbox and neatly piling all the mail on her kitchen table, Jason takes just a moment to sit down at the table, remembering how many good times they shared there. He hopes they'll be able to share more good times together soon.

Later that week, as he checks Ivy's mailbox, the only item within is a postcard. He's not trying to be nosy, but postcards are hard to ignore. He sees mountains and columbine flowers on the front and catches Ivy's name on the back, as the sender. She's written to him.

Thank you for checking my mail. I appreciate it. Toby misses you. Maybe I do too. – Ivy

He takes out his phone and types a quick message to Ivy.

JASON
Got your card, I miss Toby too. But I definitely miss you more.

By the time he's made his way back up to his apartment, Ivy has responded.

> IVY
> Glad to hear it.

JASON
Maybe we can talk when you are back in town?

> IVY
> Talk about our feelings? Sounds terrible. Let's do it.

JASON
It'll be the worst. Can't wait.

Jason considers writing more, but what he wants to tell Ivy really shouldn't be said over text. He'll be patient and wait for when she's home and ready to see him. He'll be ready to show her how committed he is to their relationship when the time comes.

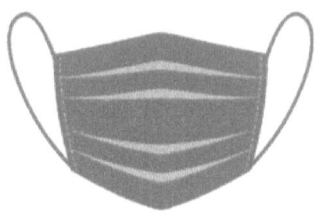

<u>CHAPTER 33</u>

Before they know it, Thanksgiving is only a few days away and it's time to think about the menu. The holiday is an opportunity to really go balls-out with the old Collins family favorites. Ivy volunteers to go to Trader Joe's on Monday to pick up all the ingredients along with an extra bag or two of "Oh! That looks good!" impulse buys while Holly stays home with Toby.

Colorado Trader Joe's aren't *real* TJ's, in Ivy's opinion. She's explained this to Holly before, but a true TJ's experience must involve the traditional terrible parking lot and not quite enough room inside to accommodate the after-work crowds. Denver TJ's have ample parking, nice wide aisles, and plenty of room for check-out lines. Unacceptable.

As Ivy stands in the line outside, waiting for shoppers to leave so new ones can go in, she soon discovers the three layers and her jacket were not enough to keep her warm longer than five minutes outside. If Holly were here, she'd most definitely be calling Ivy a wuss. Which is fair.

When Ivy first moved to Los Angeles over fifteen years ago, she would laugh when the early morning crowd would wander into the coffee shop where she worked all bundled up in their peacoats because it was only 55 degrees outside. Ivy would just smile and agree when they said it was "freezing" knowing she had walked into the shop only an hour before in a t-shirt. But now? Anything below 70 degrees is jacket weather for her.

Ivy returns to Holly's with five bags of groceries containing all but two of the items on her list (one was out of stock, one she forgot) and about a million other items that just looked too good to pass up.

Even sampling a lot of these treats daily, by the time Thanksgiving rolls around, there are still so many tasty items that it's a full day of grazing on a variety of snacks before the expansive dinner spread of meatloaf, mashed potatoes with peas, and a half dozen other side items. Dinner is complete when both sisters are so full they're legitimately concerned they might not be able to get up from their chairs and waddle over to the living room.

A few hours later, they manage to plop down onto the floor to play cards and sort-of watch Deadpool. This is another Collins family tradition. Games after dinner. There are about a half dozen card games they have played since they were kids.

Ivy wins the first game, doing a seated victory dance while she collects all the cards, then groans when she realizes she is far too full to move that much. Holly is feeling the same pain, so they decide the one game is enough for now.

They do some online Black Friday shopping the following day, but spend most of the long weekend lazily napping, snacking, and playing cards.

Before they know it, it's Monday and Ivy's trying her best not to think too much about Jason, which has been a real problem since their quick text exchange, but her first day back to work after such a lovely languid weekend makes it nearly impossible. She can't get her hopes up though. He's a nice guy, of course he'll respond nicely to her little olive branch note. That doesn't mean his feelings have changed. Especially considering they haven't communicated since.

Her audiobook, which is supposed to be distracting her, is getting boring. And so is her work. And she's been sitting for way too long on this hard chair.

So, she gets up and peeks into Holly's office area to see her bopping her head to the music playing in her earbuds. Ivy slowly reaches her hand into Holly's periphery to get her attention without startling her. It doesn't work.

"Jesus fuck!" Holly yells, as she puts her hand to her chest, the international sign for, "You scared the shit out of me!" which she also says. Holly stops the music on her phone and removes her earbuds as Toby wanders into the room to investigate the commotion.

"I'm sorry," Ivy says with a guilty laugh, "I was trying not to move too quickly so I didn't scare you." Ivy picks up Toby and snuggles him, something he doesn't actually enjoy, but will tolerate for a bit. "I'm bored. I don't want to work anymore. Work is poopy."

"Work *is* poopy," Holly agrees, "What do you want to do instead?"

"I don't know!" Ivy replies, as though she's a petulant child. "Something fun."

"Do you want to go for a drive somewhere?" Holly offers. "We're getting into a not great traffic time, but we can go pick up early dinner or something."

"I don't know. I'm fitful!"

"I can see that. Let's start by putting Toby down, he seems like he's reached his maximum tolerance there," Holly says, taking on a tone of a kindly nanny to Ivy's obnoxious child.

Ivy sets Toby gently on the ground and he immediately takes a few steps away from her and then shakes off, only to look back at her and wag his tail like he wasn't just shooting Holly "save me" eyes.

"Ooh! I know!" Holly says, "I was going through some boxes in my basement and found my old VCR and a bunch of VHS tapes including, wait for it, Sweating to the Oldies II."

"What? How could you keep this from me?" Ivy asks in mock outrage. "We *have* to do that. I wish I had brought some spandex, legwarmers, and a sweatband to workout in. If only I had known!" and she gives Holly a resentful side eye glance.

"Sorry! I wasn't *trying* to keep it from you, I just forgot. But also, those are more 80's workout clothes, I think this was early 90's."

"Hmmm, well then, I wish I had brought my Umbros? And my Chicago Bulls t-shirt?" Ivy says, trying to remember what she wore around that time.

"Yah, that seems right. Anyway, I hooked everything up and watched a few old movies, Mystic Pizza, Kickboxer, our version of The Goonies with the giant squid."

"Oh my god! You still have that? I remember in high school when I commented to a friend how dumb that break-dancing squid scene was and he had no idea what the hell I was talking about. You can never, ever, get rid of that tape. It's probably a collector's item."

"It's probably in deleted scenes on the DVD now," Holly replies.

They change into some more appropriate workout attire and go down to Holly's basement where the VCR is hooked up to her old college TV.

"This whole set up makes me so happy," Ivy says.

"You ready to sweat?" Holly asks as she hits play on the VCR.

"I'm ready to slowly move to some oldies. I'll sort of be embarrassed if I actually break a sweat," Ivy replies.

"Oh, that's teenage Ivy talking," Holly warns. "Don't get too cocky. It's quite possible that what we used to think of as barely even moving might actually leave us winded now."

Ivy can't help but smile when she sees an effervescent Richard Simmons in his teal tank top and striped short-shorts. They follow along and warm-up to "Fever", played by Richard's in-house band. Ivy looks over at Holly who is intently watching the screen. Her typical determination to master any skill written all over her face.

It soon becomes clear to both of them that even in their forties and with a few extra pounds, they are able to do the workout with minimal sweating. Even though the exercises are not particularly challenging, the fabulous cheesiness of the video improves Ivy's mood. When the workout is done, she has the added nostalgic bonus of rewinding the tape so it's at the beginning and ready to go for next time.

"I feel like we need to go have a 90's post workout drink," Ivy says.

"Like a Snapple maybe?"

"Maybe a Clearly Canadian?" Holly suggests. "Oh! New York Seltzer!"

"Yes! Peach, raspberry, or black cherry!" Ivy replies, fully enveloped in childhood memories.

They continue to list drinks and snacks they remember but since Holly does not, oddly enough, have any of the retro treats in her home, they decide to make a light dinner before sitting down to watch tv. Basically, the same they do every night.

Ivy washes the dishes left over from lunch as Holly cooks. Her wet hands still in the sink, Ivy shouts to Holly over the Garth Brooks song blaring over Holly's tiny Bluetooth speaker.

"Toss me that spatula if you're done with it, I'll wash it now."

Holly picks up the spatula and rather than throwing it to someone with soapy hands, she takes the few steps to hand it to Ivy. As she walks, Holly sings, "I'm not going to toss the spatula to the Washer, oh Valley of Plenty, oh Valley of Plenty."

"What is that from?" Ivy asks.

Holly stops and gives her a look that says "Seriously?"

"What?" Ivy laughs, not knowing what she's missing.

"You really didn't watch anything but Henry, did you?"

"Oh, is that from Witcher?" Ivy replies, guiltily.

"Yes, it was a pretty popular song that Jaskier sang. Not those exact words, of course, but if you had been paying attention, at all, even a little, you would have recognized it."

"Hey! I have admitted to only watching Henry!" Ivy replies, and Holly shakes her head at Ivy in mock disappointment. "I'm sure it was a catchy tune. I'm sure Jaskier sang it beautifully. But are you really going to try to tell me it was better than Henry?"

"No."

"And are you going to try to pretend Henry isn't the best part of that show?"

"I am not. But it's just amazing how much you missed," Holly says.

"I would actually blame my phone more than I would blame dear Henry. But either way, it'll be fun when I rewatch it one day because it'll be like a brand new show to me!"

"Way to look on the bright side," Holly replies.

With some project deadlines pushed back, Ivy is able to extend her stay into December. She was hoping to stay through the end of the year and head back the first weekend in January, but she's reached the limit of work she can do without going into the office to pick up some things.

She and Holly decide to put up the tree on the first of the month, too lazy to do it on Black Friday. This process has its ups and downs. Down: putting up Holly's Christmas tree is hell. She's had it for decades, long before trees came pre-lit which means meticulously placing each twinkle light on the seemingly millions of branches. Up: Getting to see all the old ornaments from their childhood that Holly has stored at her place.

Ivy gently unwraps the pine-scented pink and brown gingerbread man and woman, a pair of ornaments the girls received when Ivy was just a baby. The gold thread loops they each hang from have long ago frayed, but they are otherwise in perfect condition. No chips or scrapes, and their fragrance is still strong. Suspiciously strong, actually. The scent that has lasted over forty years and probably contains chemicals that have long since been outlawed.

"It just occurred to me that these should smell like gingerbread. Not pine," Ivy says to Holly as she breathes in the familiar aroma.

"Way to ruin our childhoods," Holly replies as she takes one of the ornaments from Ivy and carefully places it on the tree.

Ivy decides to officially take some vacation time so she can stretch out her visit as long as possible and really relax and enjoy the last week of her trip. They decide to move Christmas up a few days, allowing the sisters to celebrate their favorite holiday together while also missing the predicted snow and giving Ivy a long weekend to drive back and still have some time to recoup before returning to work.

On December 21st, they pretend it's Christmas Eve and spend the day baking and decorating cookies. That evening, they keep their childhood tradition of opening one present and then saving the rest for Christmas morning. Of course, they have far fewer presents now than they did as kids, but it's still fun.

On their fake Christmas day, they finish with presents and begin their movie marathon, staying in their pajamas all day, much to Toby's resentment since his walks were skipped in lieu of extra trips to the back yard. Eventually, Ivy does some laundry and starts to gather up all her stuff that has managed to spread throughout Holly's house, preparing for the drive back home. For the most part though, it's a very lazy day. Ivy just has one quick text to send.

> IVY
> Hi. Thank you for dealing with my mail for me. I'm going to be driving back tomorrow, so you won't have to check it anymore.

She sets her phone down and purposely leaves the room so she can't check it or sit around waiting for a reply. She goes to feed Toby and discusses with Holly which one of the half dozen desserts they should have.

After eating a few cookies and a huge slice of carrot cake, Ivy finally looks at her phone. She has a new message from Jason.

JASON
You're welcome. I'll leave your mail, your apartment key, and the mailbox key on your kitchen table tonight. Have a safe trip.

It's a short and simple message, but that doesn't stop Ivy from over-analyzing it. If she's being honest, she was a little, ever so slightly, just a wee bit disappointed that there isn't a lengthy apology or an attempt to win her back. She dismisses that foolish thought and focuses on him offering to return her apartment key. It's just polite, right? He probably just assumes that *she* wants the key back. He's not trying to say that he no longer wants anything to do with her, right? Was that what he wanted to talk about?

And what's that sad feeling mixed with panic she's having now? She was the one who cut things off with him. Did she think a postcard would erase the things she had said to him? Did she really think that some polite texting meant he was ready to settle down? Ivy puts down her phone, takes a deep breath and shouts to Holly in the other room.

"What alcohol do you have?"

An hour later, Holly and Ivy snuggle into their living room seats to enjoy some Fireball Whiskey spiked apple cider after their breakfast for dinner treat of lemon blueberry pancakes and bacon. They turn on *Death Comes to Pemberley*, again.

Not used to drinking and having quite a buzz on, Ivy falls asleep about five minutes after finishing her drink. She is a wild party animal, passed out by 9:15pm.

CHAPTER 34

It's time for Ivy and Toby to hit the road. Ivy really did intend to save all her favorite podcasts for the drive home. But she's weak and she needs instant gratification, so she listened to all of them as soon as they came out.

She starts their long journey home with a sweet romantic audiobook and rather than enjoying the hopeful, everything turns out perfect ending that would usually leave her in a good mood, the story just leaves her feeling bitter.

So, a few hours in, as they stop in Grand Junction to get gas, Ivy switches to *My Dad Wrote a Porno*, her go-to podcast when she needs a good laugh.

This time, her Utah hotel is far less remote than the one she and Toby stayed at on the way to Colorado. Sure, there are still an abundance of giant trucks with flags, but the hotel lacks that white supremacist vibe the other place had.

After a decent night's sleep, she and Toby are back on the road bright and early, eager to get home. With the most stressful and winding part of the trip behind them, Ivy enjoys the drive. Well, she enjoys it for the first five hours.

The last two hours are torture and have her experiencing a very strong sense of, "I need to get the fuck out of this car," no matter what she does to try to distract herself.

She calls Holly to see if chatting will help, but quickly learns she's too annoyed with SoCal traffic to maintain friendly conversation, so she lets Holly go rather than making her deal with Ivy's grump mood.

When they finally arrive back home, Ivy is so relieved that she could cry. Okay, maybe she does cry. Just a little. Not an alarming amount, but more than an eye-water.

She opens her apartment door, letting Toby walk in before her and they are greeted by the deep scent of cinnamon. She smiles when she sees her decorations. She kind of forgot how balls-out she had gone. Even though she already celebrated, she's glad that she thought of decorating before she left because her apartment feels cozy and welcoming. She'll probably just leave this all up through January.

Car unloaded, Ivy turns on the TV and wanders into the kitchen where Jason has neatly placed her mail on the table. She didn't see it before when she walked by, but she notices a handwritten note and experiences a feeling that is somewhere between excitement and nausea. Hesitantly, she picks it up and begins to read.

Hi.

I hope we can talk soon. I'm sure you're tired from your trip, but I'll be here when you're ready.

Jason

It's a short note, but Ivy conducts her now traditional over-analysis of everything having to do with Jason and reads it over and over until the words don't even make sense anymore.

Good, he really does want to talk, he wasn't just being nice. But *why* does he want to talk? Does that mean he wants his friend back, or is he ready for more? After so much time away and two long drives, Ivy has decided she can't just be his friend again. Pretending she doesn't want more than friendship is not healthy.

But then again, if he claims he wants more than friendship, she's not sure how she can really believe him after his little moment of panic. How could she trust him? Ivy takes some deep breathes and before she can overthink too much more, she decides to text him and get it over with. She'll just be honest. Well, honest but brief. Don't overdo the honesty. No pledges of love or anything, but make it clear she's open to … something.

IVY
I'm back, got your note. I still want to talk too. I'm just not quite ready yet.

Not too long later, Jason replies.

JASON
I understand, no rush. Whenever you're ready.

Back to her typical work from home quaroutine, Ivy and Toby walk down the hall to start their mid-morning walk. Ivy conducts her sneaky investigation of the packages left outside of her neighbors' doors.

People aren't in full lockdown anymore and the initial cautions that mail could spread the virus have been revoked, so packages tend not to stay in the hall as long, but it's still a fun game to play now that she's back home: who are my neighbors and what do they buy?

Apartment Six has something from Michael's, maybe she is a crafter as well as a peanut butter lover. Maybe she made the wreath on her door. Apartment One has something from Sephora. Ivy hasn't really gotten a good look at the woman who moved in there, but she guesses the woman is in her 20's. Even in a damn pandemic Apartment One always seems to be dressed cute, so makeup seems very on-brand for her.

As they get closer to the exit, Ivy hears Annie's voice coming from the lobby and considers turning around and going out the basement door when she hears Jason's voice as well. Ivy listens for a moment. It seems that he has adopted the same strategy with Annie as Ivy has, agree, answer only what is needed, try to escape. Ivy decides to save Jason rather than sneak out the back.

"Hi guys!" Ivy calls out with well-feigned enthusiasm to see them both. Then, looking at Jason, "Toby and I are headed out are you joining us today?"

Jason smiles at her and even though he's holding his mail and clearly wasn't planning on joining them, he replies with equal enthusiasm, turning to Annie to politely excuse himself, offering the perfect amount of regret to leave such a stimulating conversation.

"You two have fun!" Annie calls after them.

Outside, Toby leads them around the corner on their shortest route. Toby's excitement from seeing Jason has them all walking at a quick pace but in a somewhat awkward silence, which Jason very kindly breaks.

"Thank you for inviting me along."

"You're welcome. You don't actually have to walk with us if you need to get back. I'm sure you could sneak in through the basement entrance and miss Annie."

"No, I don't have any meetings. I'd love to walk with you guys," he says as he looks down affectionately at Toby who keeps looking back at him with mutual admiration. Ivy watches the adorable little traitor wag his tail at Jason.

"Looks like my postcard wasn't a lie, he did miss you," she says, trying for a tone that doesn't ooze too much bitterness.

"I missed him. I've missed both of you. Very much."

Ivy doesn't have a reply to this. Or maybe she has too many replies to choose just one. Either way, she doesn't say anything right away. To fill the obvious silence, she decides to aim for polite conversation.

"Did you do anything special for Christmas?" is what she goes with, figuring it's slightly better than discussing the weather.

"Just Zoomed with the family. Ordered food in. Nothing exciting."

"You didn't go visit your mom and Bill?"

"I thought about it, but I decided to stay home. I had stuff to take care of and I haven't been the best company."

"I hope you at least had some good holiday food. And watched some good Christmas movies."

"I did. I did the lonely single man Christmas dinner of kung pao chicken, cheese wontons, and mu shu pork. And I watched A Christmas Story and Home Alone. Oh, and Die Hard."

God damn it, of course he recognizes Die Hard as a Christmas classic. And fucking of course he watched her two other favorite Christmas movies. She stops herself from telling him that and, instead, just unleashes some babble at him, not even sure what she's saying.

"Those are good ones. I also like While You Were Sleeping. And though it's not actually a Christmas movie, I like watching the Winona Ryder Little Women. And Harry Potter and the Sorcerer's Stone. I guess anything that has a Christmas scene counts for me." Why is she nervous? This is Jason.

"Maybe I'll add those to my Christmas movie list next year." Then, completely and abruptly changing the topic, he continues, "You said before that I just assumed what your feelings were about us, but never asked you, which was true. So, how do you feel about me? What do *you* want from our relationship?"

Ivy's stomach drops but she manages to force out a laugh and a choked, "Wow."

"I know that was a lot. I just had to put that out there. Don't answer now, take as much time as you need, but I really want to discuss that when you're ready to tell me. Also, I wanted to let you know that I'm moving."

"You're throwing a lot of information at me. Okay. Wow. Where are you going? When are you leaving? Congrats!" Ivy manages to make her congratulations sound sincere while also panicking at the thought of him not being nearby.

"I found a place in a good area that needed a little work, but my friend's crew was available so they've been working on it. It's ready for me to move in. But, I'm not telling you that to rush you. Let me know when you're ready to meet. Dinner, lunch, another walk, coffee, whatever you want."

She considers replying, "I think you said enough the last time we spoke," but before she can say anything, she feels her stupid eyes start to fill with stupid tears. Damn it! First Toby betrays her, now her eyes? Hey anus, do you want to get in on the embarrassment? Let's make this moment *really* uncomfortable.

"No, we should talk before you move."

"Great. I'll text you later this week so we can figure out a time," Jason says before he gives Toby a parting pat on the head and scratch behind the ear. "I'll let you guys go. See you later."

As soon as Ivy and Toby are inside their apartment, she calls Anthony. The second he answers, before he can even get his full "Hello" out, Ivy blurts out, "Toby and I were heading outside and Jason was in the lobby trapped by Annie and so I helped him escape and invited him to walk with us and he told me he's moving and wants to talk to me. Which I already knew, the talking, not the moving, because he left me a note asking to talk but I was putting it off because I can't take it if he says any more disappointing shit to me, but he was so nice and he smelled good and he looked me in the eyes and he was happy to see Toby too and I couldn't say no, so I told him I would meet him. But I'm wondering if I should have done that. Maybe I should cancel."

Without missing a beat, Anthony replies to that tsunami of prattle. "Why are you wondering that?"

"I'm trying to learn from my mistakes and not pursue men who don't actually want to be with me."

"Hmm."

"What does 'hmm' mean?" Ivy asks.

"From what you told me, it sounded like he needed time to work on himself, but it never sounded like he didn't have feelings for you. Plus, you never mentioned feeling that imbalance with him that you've mentioned with other men."

"Okay. Yes. This isn't the same exact problem I've had in past relationships, but doesn't it leave us in the same place? He can't make a romantic commitment. And us just being friends left me feeling like shit."

"It's been a couple of months, maybe he's figured some things out."

"Maybe," Ivy concedes, cautiously.

"Look, all I'm saying is that you guys seemed to really be getting along before …"

"The unfortunate incident," Ivy offers.

"Yes, that. Dustin and I were fully expecting you to bring him over so we could meet him, judge him, and give our stamp of approval. That's serious. So, I don't think it's a bad idea to listen to what he has to say. I don't think he'd ask to talk just to tell you he's not interested in you."

"True. Unless he's hoping I'm the one to say we should just be friends so he can agree and not look like a dick."

"If I had to guess, I would say this is going to be an apology and maybe even a begging situation. The men you're trying to equate Jason to haven't done that before, so it might be fair to say he's not like the other men you've dated," Anthony asserts.

"Well, yah, and we weren't actually dating. We were friends."

"Which is also different because I don't know that you actually liked some of the men you've dated."

Ivy takes a moment to think this over. Is that true? Oh my god, she thinks, that *is* true.

"My advice is to talk to him, with an open mind. Don't go into it dreading it or thinking of ways to get out of it or shorten it or whatever."

"I was thinking about pulling the 'I got a text from my neighbor. Toby is howling, I'd better go back' plan," Ivy says, partially joking.

"That's easily debunked though since he lives in your building and might head back with you."

"Yah, I mean, it wasn't my *best* escape plan."

"Look," Anthony continues, getting them back on track. "You're not committing to anything by hearing him out. What you decide to do after that is up to you."

"I guess."

"Let's just say, hypothetically, I'm right and he's going to apologize and profess his undying love for you," Anthony says. "How would you feel about that?"

"Uhhhhhgg. I don't know!" Ivy moans in a fake cry. "In theory, that would be wonderful. But I would have trouble believing him because not that long ago, he said he wanted to have sex too, but then he freaked. So, I can't really trust anything he says when it comes to feelings."

"I still think it's a good idea to hear him out. If it goes horribly bad, you can fully blame me."

"Oh, I will."

CHAPTER 35

Ivy and Jason make plans to walk to Starbucks together and then sit at the park for their official talk. The trip to Starbucks isn't too bad, the small talk is not quite as easy as usual, but Ivy tells him about her time in Colorado to fill the void. Jason listens but doesn't really offer any more details about what he did during their time apart.

By the time they reach the park and sit down at an open picnic table, some of the tension between them has evaporated.

"I had a job where they called these sorts of serious talks 'courageous conversations'," Ivy says.

Jason forces a laugh and says, "Look, you know I'm not a fan of talking about feelings either, but I do need to tell you some things and I want to know how you're feeling about everything."

"I've thought a lot about us, but you go first."

"OKAY. The day after our ..." and he trails off a bit as he searches for a gentle word to describe their emotional brawl.

"Unfortunate incident," Ivy offers.

Jason nods and continues, "I still had a lot of shame and guilt about what I did, but mostly, I had the very real feeling that I wasn't going to see you again. And that made me miserable."

After a moment, Ivy says, begrudgingly, "I don't like how things are between us right now either."

"I want you to know that I really care about you. The fact that I care about you so much is *why* I panicked," and seeing the look on Ivy's face, he continues, "I know you don't believe that. But it's true. It scared me because I wasn't ready to deal with the possibility of having my heart broken again. It was not, and I can't emphasize this enough, because I regretted sleeping with you. I hope you can believe that."

Ivy looks down at her cup while she takes this in. If she ignores the part of her brain telling her she's not good enough, the part that tells her all her failed relationships have really been her fault because she does not deserve to be loved in the way she wants, and she thinks about how things were between them, she can honestly see that what Jason is saying could be true.

"I guess I can believe that," she says.

"I don't want there to be any confusion about what I want. I want us to date. That's going to look a lot like what we were doing, watching tv, having meals together, doing nothing together, because I just like being around you. But then I'm hoping for a lot more cuddling, making out, and sex."

Ivy smiles at him. "I've done nothing but think about us since ... "

"My horrible response to a wonderful thing," Jason offers.

Ivy nods and says, "I don't think I could go back to us being friends, so I'm happy you want more. But here's my problem, and you probably think I'm harping on this, but I can't let it go. When you left that night, I was so hurt because I genuinely didn't expect that coldness from you. I never thought you could treat me like that and it made me second guess our friendship and what I thought I knew about you. So, while I can accept that your panic was not from regret, and I love hearing you say you want more, how do I know it won't happen again the next time things get serious?"

Jason reaches out to grab one of her hands folded on the table in front of her. He holds it and looks her in the eyes. "I fucked up. But I'm clear on what I want now. I want to be with you. I *want* things to get serious with us. I'm ready to be serious again."

Ivy, of course, begins to cry. "I am very happy to hear you say that. And I guess I'll just have to trust you. But you should know, if you make me feel like that again, I'll fucking kill you."

Jason laughs and squeezes her hand. "I believe you. I would deserve it. And hey, you owe me one terrible, awful, gut-wrenching mistake that I have to forgive you for. So that's got to take a lot of pressure off you."

"I never thought of it that way. That is pretty cool."

He's so relieved that he seriously considers pulling a Tom Cruise jumping on Oprah's couch moment on this picnic table.

"Come here," Jason says as he stands and helps Ivy out from the bench and onto her feet. He hugs her, holding her next to him and she hugs him back, happy to be with him again. "I'm going to show you that I'm serious about us."

"Good. I look forward to it," Ivy says into his neck.

"Will you take a walk with me?"

Ivy pulls away to look at him, her eyebrows knit with confusion. "Uh, I guess? Where?"

"I have a surprise for you. I was going to wait a while, but I think this might be the right time. And I totally deserve that look you're giving me, but will you come with me?"

Ivy realizes her brows are heavily furrowed, giving away her confusion. She tries to give a more open expression, and Jason smiles at her. Taking her hand, he tosses their cups in the trash and enthusiastically leads her out of the park and up the sidewalk back toward their building.

"Are we going back to your place?" Ivy asks, still unsure what he has planned. His obvious excitement is adorable enough that she forgives him being so cagey. "Are you about to ravish me?"

"Ha! Not quite yet," Jason replies, inwardly thinking maybe that would be a better idea. It's too late for that right now. He's committed to revealing his surprise. But, stopping in the middle of the sidewalk, he turns toward her, pulls down his mask, then hers, and kisses her. Ivy's not usually one for

PDA, but those hesitations are fleeting as she's quickly reminded of how nice it is to kiss him.

The wall she built up around her heart in their time apart crumbles completely as they pull apart and Ivy sees how genuinely happy Jason is. Happy to be with *her*.

"Come on," Jason says, and continues to guide her up the sidewalk. They do not, however, go into their building.

"Are we not going to your apartment?" Ivy asks.

"Nope. Keep going!"

They walk into the fancy neighborhood they both like so much and soon Ivy finds herself outside of a large two-story craftsman house as Jason takes her up the inviting front path and unlocks the door, leading her inside.

"Let me show you around."

Ivy is first hit with the strong scent of paint mixed with fresh cut wood, but is able to take a quick glance around to appreciate how cute it is before Jason excitedly moves her quickly to the rear of the house to a room off the kitchen. It's a mudroom with two doors to the outside. Jason steps into the room and gestures to a doggie door in one of the doors.

"This one leads to the dog run," Jason says. "If you go out that door," he points to the door across from them, "It'll take you to the backyard."

They step outside using the door to the run and Ivy finds herself standing in a fully enclosed dog run, just like she imagined. She can envision Toby having a great time when they visit, fully protected from any wild animals as he sniffs, runs, and barks at nothing.

"Oh, that's not all," Jason says. "Come on."

He eagerly guides her back inside and then up the stairs to the second floor where she sees a small nook with a stained-glass window to her right, a perfect place to read or, more realistically for her, scroll through TikTok. There are two doors, one at each end of a hallway. Before Jason takes her to what Ivy assumes must be his bedroom, he looks her straight in the eyes and says, "This is our bedroom. Well, bedroom*s*."

Ivy registers the words "our bedroom" and it all becomes clear to her, this isn't Jason just putting some of her ideas in his home. This is *their* home. Her lingering reservations about him not really being ready for a commitment fly right out the beautiful stained-glass window.

The room is a decent size with large windows and a lot of natural light. It has the standard craftsman woodwork around the doors and windows, but otherwise, is fairly plain. The connected bathroom has a large shower, a separate toilet, two sinks, and plenty of counter space. A pair of small leaded windows offer more light to the bright space.

"I was thinking this room would be mine, but whichever one you want, it's yours. The walk-in closet connects them and it's just through here," he says as he crosses the room and opens what appeared to be built in shelves with lower cabinet doors, but what is actually…

"A secret door!" Ivy gasps. "And it's not depressing hidden annex-y at all!"

"Yah, I thought it being built in and having the cabinet doors gave it a normal craftsman vibe. I'm glad you agree."

Ivy doesn't respond because she's too busy being stunned by the enormous closet complete with shoe racks and laundry hamper nooks.

"Oh my god, it's amazing!" Ivy says.

"I let my friend design it. He gave you all the most popular requests he gets for fancy closets."

"It's perfect," Ivy replies as she takes in the details, knowing that she doesn't actually have enough clothes, shoes, or jewelry to fill up even a third of this massive space. But she welcomes the challenge.

The secret door is a mirror on the inside of the closet and there's an identical one across from it. Jason confirms her suspicion. "That's another secret door that leads into your room."

She looks at him with true wonder and he can't help but laugh.

"Go ahead, check it out, see how you like it," he tells her and Ivy squeals in response.

As soon as she sees her room, she can tell Jason designed it just for her. It has more attention to detail than the other room.

"I didn't change much downstairs, but this second story isn't part of the original house, so I didn't feel bad about gutting it. But I did also want it to match the rest of the house, so I had them do built-ins like the ones in the living room, which I'll show you when we go back downstairs. And the windows match the original ones in the dining room, I thought you'd like that."

Still processing everything, Ivy is only able to get out another, "It's amazing."

She walks over to the bookcases flanking each side of a built-in seat under a large window with smaller leaded windows on each side. She opens the glass doors to the bookcase, which match the windows above. Then she sits down on the window seat and looks up at Jason, speechless.

"Don't forget to check out your bathroom." He takes her hand and leads her into the bathroom which is slightly larger than his to allow for a clawfoot tub.

"I know you're not that into baths, but it's nice and deep if you ever want to indulge. Plus, you can bathe Toby in there."

"It's so pretty. It's better than I imagined."

"There's one last thing I wanted to show you." Still holding her hand, he leads Ivy out her bedroom door into the hall, and back downstairs to the living room. He rushed her through so quickly when they first came in, she didn't really see anything. Now, they stop in front of the fireplace which has a large framed picture over it and as soon as she sees it, Ivy begins to cry.

"Oh my god! That's at the park!" she ekes out as she stares up at a photo of her laughing with Toby in her lap and Harry standing by watching them happily. "I didn't know you took a picture of us!"

Jason sees the big smile on her face, tears running down her cheeks and puts his arm around her waist, pulling her close to him. "I'm so glad you like all of this. I figured there was about a 20% chance that this could come off as really creepy, especially if we weren't on the same page," he says with an anxious laugh. "But that was a risk I was willing to take."

Ivy sort of snorts as a reply and wipes her tears away. "Luckily for you, I'm super shallow and totally into you for your money and this house. So, it all worked out."

Jason chuckles and holds her a little closer. "Most women want me for my giant penis, so this is a nice change for me."

Ivy laughs. "Sorry, it's both for me."

Jason turns her toward him, pulling her close to his chest. "I have something I need to tell you."

Ivy's heart races and she tenses slightly in his arms, having waited to hear these words from him for a while now.

"Annie and Otto never dated. Otto moved because the building across the street is owned by a friend who gave him a break on the rent, though the passed away ten years ago so Otto now pays the low end of market rent. Otto said he didn't mind Annie as the building manager because she was always on top of things. Annie said Otto was a good tenant, nothing more."

"Oh my god, you interrogated them?" Ivy asks as she pulls away slightly to look him in the face.

"I did. For you. Unfortunately, Annie didn't give up much info. I do sort of think she had a crush on him. But she might also just be bitter that he never has Hildy on a leash, she does love rules."

"True," Ivy agrees as she puts her head back on Jason's chest.

"I have something else to tell you." He notices that she's not tense this time, probably convinced now that he's never going to say the words he knows she needs to hear. "I knew I loved you the moment I saw you in that fucking painter's outfit. But, I was scared. And I almost let that keep me from you. Luckily, I got my head out of my ass and I know what I want. I want to spend the rest of my life with you. If you'll have me."

"I think every declaration of love and devotion should include the words 'head out of my ass'," Ivy answers back, causing Jason to laugh out loud.

"I am quite the poet," Jason replies.

Ivy steps back from him just long enough to kiss him. She tries to convey all the emotions she's feeling, tries to make sure he knows she feels the same way he feels. She pulls back again to look at him.

"I love you so fucking much."

Jason smiles at her. "Aw, you're a poet too."

They both have tears in their eyes and Ivy gives him one more deep kiss before taking her phone from her back pocket. "What are your plans for the rest of the day?"

Jason, taken aback, says, "No plans. Just winning you back and professing my love for you in a grand gesture that has been months in the making."

"Good! So, since that's done, and it went really, really well by the way, you're free now?"

"I guess. I was sort of hoping for some make-up sex, but yes. I'm free for whatever you're thinking."

"Oh the sex will definitely happen, but first let me just check on something," Ivy says as she taps on Anthony's number. Jason can faintly hear the ringing and then the voice of someone saying hello on the other end. Ivy replies into her phone, "Hey, when are you guys available to meet Jason?"

www.ingramcontent.com/pod-product-compliance
Lightning Source LLC
Chambersburg PA
CBHW031729170626
46808CB00005B/1943